FEMALE GENITAL MUTILATION IN AFRICA

Gender, Religion and Pastoral Care

by Daniel Njoroge Karanja

Female Genital Mutilation in Africa
by Daniel Njoroge Karanja

Printed in the United States of America

ISBN 1-591605-61-X

Unless otherwise indicated, Bible quotations are taken from the *New International Version of the Bible.* Copyright © 1984, B.B. Kirkbride Bible Co., Inc, Indianapolis, Indiana and The Zondervan Corporation, Grand Rapids, Michigan, U.S.A.

Xulon Press
www.XulonPress.com

Xulon Press books are available in bookstores everywhere, and on the Web at www.XulonPress.com.

DEDICATION

*To all survivors and victims of
harmful cultural practices in Africa.*

FOREWORD

This book is timely. Fortunately, the Kenyan media is manifesting a new openness to discussing female genital mutilation. There could not be a more important topic.

If the Christian faith community in Kenya, and in Africa, is to establish and maintain its relevance, it must address this oppressive and demeaning cultural practice. The voice of the Church is powerful and respected. African theologians will make their Christian faith authentically African by addressing thorny issues that face Africa today. Cultural and tribal practices that discriminate and harm women are among the most important. Female genital mutilation is an extreme, inhuman and traumatic form of violence against innocent girls and women. As African theologians relate the Christian gospel to the African context, they are by definition involved in educating people, men and women alike, to the Scriptures' message of radical liberation. As African theologians and ministers engage in this liberating education, they must remember that female genital mutilation concerns the physical, emotional, psychological and spiritual well being of their beloved sisters, daughters and wives.

This work is an invitation and a challenge for the faith community to continue with more research. Such research will help in the elimination of female genital mutilation. Since this is a traditional and cultural belief deeply ingrained in a people's way of life, it will take consistent and patient educational efforts from Africans to dislodge it. It is especially noteworthy that an African male theologian is taking the stand that he takes in this book. His work is relevant to pastoral counselors, nurses, midwives, pastors, theological students, teachers and college lecturers. Public policy makers and non-governmental organizations will also find this book useful.

I have known the author since the early days of his research in 1998. His boldness in addressing this subject is commendable. His work deserves careful consideration among those who seek to understand harmful practices against women and what the community of faith can do to respond.

I enthusiastically endorse and commend this excellent and important contribution of the Rev. Dr. Daniel Njoroge Karanja, *Female Genital Mutilation in Africa: Gender, Religion and Pastoral Care.*

Demaris Wehr, Ph.D.
Andover Newton Theological School
210 Herrick Road, Newton Center,
Massachusetts 02459-2243

ACKNOWLEDGEMENTS

I am grateful to God, who has enabled me to undertake this research. His grace and mercy have been sufficient. I am also thankful Dr. Demaris S. Wehr who believed in my project and affirmed the urgency of the message in this book. Her encouragement and reviewing of many drafts is sincerely appreciated. To Dr. Allie Perry and Dr. Earl Thompson for their candid feedback during the writing of this project, thank you. I am grateful to the unnamed young Kenyan girl who shared her story of pain and agony in attempting to escape from the cruel hands of family members attempting to mutilate her. God's grace be with her.

I am also thankful to *Maendeleo Ya Wanawake* Organization of Kenya for their relentless efforts in fighting for the rights of women in Kenya. They also provided some helpful data from the organization's archives.

Thanks to the editorial staff at Xulon Press in Florida, USA, for their hard work and efficiency to produce this magnificent book.

Finally, I thank my family especially my spouse, Joyce, for putting up with me and persevering through hours of gruesome pictures and materials that seemed to be "unholy." Her prayers, inspiration and constant encouragement made this work possible. To our children, Wanjiku, Karanja and Gitahi, who persevered many hours without me, taking away quality time from them as I worked on this manuscript. You have been very kind to me and I salute you all.

TABLE OF
CONTENTS

INTRODUCTION

I cannot go home." Violet sighed, with tears streaming down her face. It was in August 1991, time for the school holidays, and Violet hated it. Back home, near Meru town in Eastern Kenya, her family had finalized all the plans for her to undergo female genital mutilation. There was no place to hide; close and distant relatives alike approved of the practice. I listened to Violet with frustration and disappointment knowing that I had no answer for her. As I prayed to the Lord for mercy on Violet, I became very much aware of my own hopelessness and helplessness in this situation. I never heard from her again. I have always wondered what happened to her. Violet is one among millions of innocent girls who face the cruelty of female genital mutilation in Africa today.

The author will use the term female genital mutilation in place of female circumcision because the latter term makes it sound more ritualistic than a cruel and violent treatment of innocent girls carried out in secrecy and silence. The author believes that female genital mutilation is a deeply rooted tribal practice supported and sustained by women and men who strongly believe that it's a requirement to mark the transition from childhood to adulthood.

The surprising silence by the communities of faith in the midst of the suffering of innocent girls reveals the discomfort around this subject, especially among Christians. Ironically enough, there is no outcry against the innocent lives that are destroyed daily under the guise of culture and tradition. In 1967, the United Nations passed the declaration on the elimination of discrimination against women. In 1975, the same organization passed another declaration on the protection of all persons from torture. These documents have had no impact in protecting the victims of female genital mutilation. The suffering continues. The author believes that the battle against the practice can be won through long and short-term goals involving, first and foremost, religious communities because they have direct access to the victims and perpetrators. Non-governmental organizations and government efforts might supplement these efforts.

The author invites you to join him in examining the physical, psychological and theological aspects of female genital mutilation. Kenya will be the specific country of reference while other African countries will be highlighted.

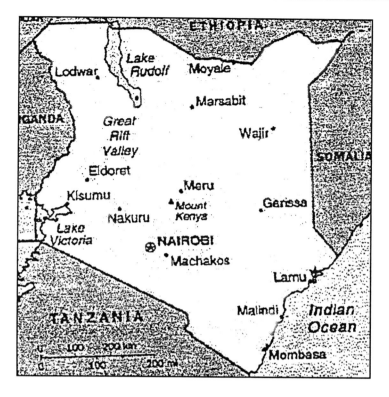

MAP OF KENYA

*Tourist map of Kenya by courtesy of Kenya Publishers
Limited, Nairobi, Kenya, 1996*

DEFINITIONS

The practice about to be described has permanent traumatic consequences in the lives of its victims.[1] Female genital mutilation is 'any definitive and irremediable removal of a healthy organ in the female genitalia.[2] Referring to female genital mutilation, as a harmless ritualistic rite of passage masks the real brutality of this heinous act. Most tribal communities in Africa label the mutilation as circumcision, minimizing the impact of the cruel cutting of extremely sensitive private parts of an innocent and helpless girl. The naming of the practice is important in the dialogue especially among young men and women who are more courageous to openly talk about sexuality issues than the elderly.

There are four types of female genital mutilations: first, clitoridectomy, the cutting of the entire vaginal area and parts of the clitoris; second, excision, the removal of the clitoris is carried out to include parts of the labia minora exposing the vaginal introitus and the urethra; third, intermediate infibulation which involves the severe cutting of the clitoris and the labia minora. Stitching is completed leaving a larger posterior opening for urine and menstrual flow. Fourth, total infibulation whereby all the above steps are carried out and includes total extraction of the entire clitoris, labia majora and a thorough stitching that covers the vagina and the urethra. A very small opening is left for menstrual flow and urine. [3]

The World Health Organization (WHO) adds to the definitions, by stating that there are other torturous methods that include piercing, burning and introducing foreign objects in the vaginal area, and they all fall under the definition of female genital mutilation given above.[4]

Mutilating girls meets no known need and "...there is absolutely no reason, medical, moral, or aesthetic, to suppress all or any part of these exterior genital organs."[5]

Female genital mutilation permanently damages the lives of young women and children. FGM supporters strongly believe that it is a cultural requirement. The fact that some women have fully embraced this practice and advocate for its continuity is shocking and goes against common sense and understanding. However, the author trusts that this work will raise cultural educational awareness and expose the dangers of tribal and religious myths associated with the practice.

The empowerment process to enable its eradication will be rooted in education, pastoral care, advocacy and comprehensive research. FGM ranks high as one of the worst forms of sexual abuse, child abuse and exploitation in the name of culture and tradition. The psychological trauma resulting from this mutilation is yet to be scientifically measured. A permanent sense of loss, shame, guilt, humiliation, deprivation and trauma will be discussed later in the book. The traumatic impact can result in permanent consequences in victims.[1]

The pastoral care needs of survivors and victims will be explored. The author believes that gender specific pastoral care resources will be effective if made available and accessible to all the victims. The communities of faith in Africa seem to be insensitive to the pastoral care needs of the innocent girls and victims. The culture of silence at the center of all the suffering and hurting girls can be viewed as an indirect endorsement of the practice. Male domination, rooted in tribal and cultural beliefs, does not seem to be sensitive to the entrapment of helpless girls. Unfortunately among some communities, women are in charge of this practice and not men.

African clergy persons must step out by faith today and do whatever is within their power to dismantle all the cultural and tribal structures that have kept innocent girls and women in bondage. The cultural chains of female genital mutilation must be broken, granting freedom to the captives. Like the Old Testament Moses facing the Egyptian Pharaoh, it is time for all women and men of faith to sound off in one accord, "Let my people go!"

The redemption and liberation process will start with firing the first shot in this battle through initiating fundamental and constructive educational dialogue among religious communities in Africa. For how long can they stand by the sidelines as our sisters are tortured and abused in the name of culture and tribal loyalty? Let the battle begin in earnest now.

The immediate challenge in this type of work is the fact that there are few written research resources in the field, but that will not be an excuse or a barrier to digging out the truth wherever it may be found. Stories, songs, drama and libraries can be great sources to all those who believe in the freedom of innocent and helpless girls. No stone should be left unturned.

Why Mutilate Innocent Girls?

Gender relations among the Gikuyu community, like other communities in Africa, position the male in a superior role and the female in an inferior role. Boys were empowered and trained early in life to take positions of power and authority, leaving the girls behind as followers. From the traditional perspective, a newly married man who did not batter his wife was considered weak and cowardly. Battering one's spouse was regarded as a healthy normal practice. The painful truth is that this is still true among many communities in rural Africa, while most urban areas are changing, thanks to education and open mindedness of younger generations. Power and control of women by men in the name of cultural norms is another form of harmful practice that encourages FGM.

The primary explanation for mutilating girls among the Gikuyu community was to *make them marriageable*. It was common knowledge among the Gikuyu that a *mature man* only married a *mature woman,* where mature means a *circumcised* man and a *mutilated* woman. False propaganda about female genital mutilation was communicated through songs and oral narratives to instill fear among men who dared to consider marrying a woman who had not been mutilated. An un-mutilated girl was ridiculed, shamed in public and even ostracized, rejected and marked as not fit for marriage. Ultimately she would live in shame, in hiding for the rest of her life.

On the other hand, a mutilated woman fetched a high bridal price paid to the father in terms of livestock and locally brewed liquor. Treating women like trade commodities must be erased among humankind. The bridal price practice continues to this day, and the author suggests a thorough review of this practice. Voluntary exchange of gifts and presents among the two families joining together through marriage would build more harmony and long lasting friendships than setting monetary figures as to how much a young man will pay in terms of a bride price. The monetary aspect of it sets the wrong tone of financial greed, leaving behind a trail of resentment long after the wedding is over and unfortunately sometimes throughout the marriage. The bride price factor becomes the basis of many physical fights in the marriage, sometimes ending it.

The present generation in the year 2003 can do better than the past generations. Women are not goods for trade and the time for action is now. Female genital mutilation can no longer be used as the criteria for marriage. One of the theories behind this practice was that a mutilated woman would have a controlled sexual appetite and not seek sexual relations outside marriage. Male control over female sexuality is the prime suspect for the continuation of this inhuman and barbaric torture against innocent girls.

For example according to media reports, a sect group known as *mungiki* has renewed calls for mutilating girls and women in Central Kenya. The FGM worldwide website states that mutilation on girls was performed, "to terminate or reduce feelings of sexual arousal in women."[6] The website further lists the following ten myths commonly used to justify the mutilations:

1. It is a rite of passage and proof of adulthood.
2. It raises her status in the community through demonstrated bravery.
3. Positive character is instilled, including submission and pain endurance.
4. The initiate enjoys the attention, gifts and moral instruction.
5. It creates a comradeship and sisterhood among all women.
6. It eliminates lustful thoughts and temptation to masturbate.
7. It instills purity and preservation for marriage.
8. It affirms and strengthens the bond of marriage because the wife has never had sex with anyone else.
9. It eliminates the possibility of rape because women will not tempt men.
10. Men will be confident of their fatherhood since they are the only partners, especially where infibulation or pharaonic (a type of mutilation performed in Egypt) circumcision is done.[7]

The above myths are clearly from the perpetrators perspective, both men and women. The victim is voiceless. The element of violence and the permanent damage caused to innocent girls dismisses all the above myths. Four out of the ten myths above, have something to do with male control over women's sexuality. However, the fact that women advocates of FGM seem to be more aggressive and adamant about it, raises more questions and answers as to the origin and sustenance of this practice.

Research study completed in 1974 states that the upland Bantu tribes and the highland plain Nilotes performed female genital mutilation.[8] This practice was widespread beyond the Bantu boundaries to other people like the Cushites. Before recorded history, FGM existed among different tribes that used the practice as a way of punishing conquerors during inter-tribal conflicts.[9] Some members of the medical community in the West argued that FGM was carried out as a cure for masturbation.[10]

Among the Gikuyu community, mutilation was viewed as a cleansing ritual in a religious fashion. The Gikuyu god received animal sacrifices in the process of purifying the victims off their childhood "messes." In an interview conducted by the author in Gatura village, Thika District in central Kenya, the informant stated that the premutilation ceremonial aspects of the practice were of equal importance with the literal cutting of the flesh. Each candidate was required to have a sponsor who would have had the same capacity and influence as a godparent, in a religious sense, during baptism. The sponsor would assume the role of a counselor and guardian for the victim. While this is a noble idea to have a counselor or guardian, it does not have to be based in such a violent act against innocent girls.

Chapter 1

GENDER RELATIONS AND FEMALE GENITAL MUTILATION

"Women need judicial, political, economic and theological power to enjoy the rights promised them by God. And this is what the Churches are most afraid of..."

The Rev. Dr. Timothy Murere Njoya

M yths, narratives and proverbs from several tribes in Kenya show that women have been treated like objects for generations. For example, among the Gikuyu community, boys were socialized in a way that suggested superior habits over girls. In this section, the author attempts to demonstrate how cultural and tribal male attitudes have shaped, influenced and perpetuated violence against women. May the reader judge for herself and himself what these gender biases have contributed to the continuation of female genital mutilation and other forms of violence against women in Africa.

The following ten attitudes prevalent in the Kenyan society demonstrates the male-female attitudes that demean women. These attitudes can potentially lead to violent treatment against women. Male personal opinion indirectly influences public policy. Public policy becomes the standard to be followed by society:

Personal Male Opinion	Public Policy
1. A woman's place is in the home.	*Only hire a woman worker if there are no men available for the job.*
2. Women have nimble fingers.	*A woman's place is on the assembly line or at the typewriter*
3. Women are highly emotional and cry when they're upset.	*Keep women out of managerial positions.*
4. Women are nurturing; they love to take care of others	*Women wanted for the following positions: secretary, nurse, waitress.*
5. Women's salaries are supplementary; their husbands earn money to support the family	*If a woman is hired we can pay her less.*
6. Women are undependable. They frequently miss work because of home and child responsibilities.	*Hire women as part-time or contract workers. That way we need not pay benefits or provide job development.*

7. *All women want to get married and raise families.*

Don't waste time or money training women for greater responsibilities.

8. *Women are not team players; they don't know how to negotiate or operate by business rules.*

Keep women in inside jobs. Don't put them in positions of importance where they will represent the organization.

9. *Women know how to take orders;they are accustomed to this from their husbands, brothers and fathers.*

There is no need to consult women about the work they do; direct them, tell them what to do.

10. *Outspoken, self-confident women are troublemakers.*

Hire docile, subservient women without much self-confidence[1]

The above gender discrimination tendencies are not unique to Kenya but are evident in different expressions worldwide. They demonstrate that in male dominated communities the place and role of women is consciously and unconsciously dictated by gender-based biases. Proverbs and poems illustrate similar themes of male domination and attitudes that promote and sustain oppressive and demeaning treatment of women. In a poem entitled *"You Woman[2]"* the poet describes the treatment of women as beasts of burden among the Gikuyu community. The *Mukwa* refers to a tough and strong cord made out of sisal that women use to carry heavy loads of firewood, food, water, animal feed and groceries. The cord eventually makes a dent on the woman's head. The male in this poem mocks and insults women, observing that women in rural Africa work like donkeys or camels. Poverty and survival drives the caring mothers to do whatever they can to feed their families. Unfortunately, their industriousness and resilient attitude to provide for their families is not recognized, affirmed or appreciated.

Male chauvinism and domination of women is unjust, inhuman and a breeding ground of domestic violence. African poets and artists have in the past done an excellent job in drawing the reader's attention to the powerlessness, oppression and abuse of the African women, especially with their indescribable physical workload. Across the continent of Africa, imbalance between women and men when it comes to manual labor is outright abusive.

The male in the house expects full service by his wife. Her duties in some African countries require her to draw water from the river, carry it home, haul firewood into the house, obtain food from the garden, cook it, serve the food, and clean the dishes without any assistance. The male in the house idles around the village shopping centers doing nothing and upon his return expects full service. His wife is more of a live-in servant than a mutual partner in marriage and family life. This type of domestic exploitation and inconsiderate behavior even among Christians is ungodly, inhuman and evil; it must be eradicated. Sin is not an African cultural practice. Sin is a rebellious choice, in this case by men against women, and God is not pleased. God gave men a friend, comrade, partner, lover who is entitled to mutual happiness and shared struggles and joys in marriage, not a waitress or servant to be exploited and abused.

Gender Stereotypes in Proverbs

The following eighteen Gikuyu proverbs humiliate and objectify women. They plant the seeds of inferior attitudes and mistreatment of women by men. They promote sexism and gender discrimination. Each proverb appears in the Gikuyu language followed by a literal translation and a brief commentary.

1. *Aka eri ni nyungu cia urogi.*
Two wives are two pots of poison.

The proverb suggests that when two women come together, they are like two pots full of poison. Gossip, rumors and other antisocial behaviors dominate their time. You cannot trust two women in the same place. Watch your back, be cautious and suspicious whenever you are around women.

2. **Aka matiri cia ndiiro no cia nyiniko**
    Women have no upright words, but only crooked ones.

    Women have no integrity and cannot be depended on to keep their word.

3. **Aka na ng'ombe itiri ndugu.**
    Women and oxen have no friends

    Women, like the estranged oxen in the herd, are unfriendly and antisocial.

4. **Gia aka gitiikagio kiarara**
    A woman's word can only be trusted after the outcome

    If a woman gives you her word, you cannot trust it; wait until the outcome.

5. **Gutiri mutumia wenjagirwo mbui kwa nyina.**
    No married woman will have her white hair shaved at her mother's house.

    Marriage is permanent. No woman should ever consider divorce and returning to her parents house. She will not go into her old age living in her mother's household. Women were born to be married off.

6. **Haaro ni ya muuka uri thiiri.**
    Quarrelsome is peculiar to the woman who is in debt.

    Beware of women who are in debt; avoid lending them money.

7. **Irigukuura iriagwo iguuku ni aka.**
   The hump of the ox that has grown old is fed to women.

The massive fat in an ox's hump is found in certain breeds of cows in Africa, especially in the semi-desert areas. The proverb associates the valueless nature of the hump with that of a woman. She has no status.

8. **Kaana karere ni ucuwe gatingirungika.**
   The baby nursed by its grandmother can never be corrected.

While grandmothers are generally viewed as spoilers of little children and poor disciplinarians as suggested by this proverb, they do not permanently damage children by their love. On the contrary, they boost the child's self esteem, self worth and demonstrate the value of unconditional love.

9. **Kungu maitu na hunyu wake.**
   Long live my mother and her ugliness.

This is a demeaning and scoffing statement to one's own mother.

10. **Marakara ma arume matituraga to ma aka.**
   Men's anger does not last so long as women's.

Women have a short temper but men don't; they are well controlled.

11. **Muici na mundu muuka atigaga kieha akua.**
   He who robbed in company with a woman will live in fear until she dies.

Women cannot be trusted to keep any secrets. If you do something in secrecy with a woman, you have reason to worry until she is dead.

12. *Mundu muuka ndaigaga hitho.*
A woman cannot keep a secret.

Don't you dare share any secrets with women; they will come out.

13. *Muka mucangacangi ndagaga mwana.*
A woman that hangs about does not lack children.

A woman who sleeps around (sexual promiscuity) will not avoid getting pregnant. Women have no morals. Once more, the holier-than-thou male attitude shamefully subjects women to ridicule. It takes a man's involvement for pregnancy, and to say the least, men are immoral too.

14. *Mundu muuka na iguru itimenyagirwo.*
Women and sky cannot be understood.

Women are mysterious and unpredictable.

15. *Mundu muuka ndatumagwo thiri-ini.*
A woman is not sent to collect debts.

Women cannot be trusted with money, they may be too soft to collect the debt. Avoid involving women in financial matters.

16. *Mutumia na kionje ni undu umwe.*
A woman and a disabled person are the same.

This is a direct insult to women and the disabled community.

17. *Mutumia ndaturaga mutwe na ndaikagia ndaahi ndua.*

A woman does not split the head of a goat or dip the cup into the beer barrel.

Arrogant Gikuyu men forbid women from some chores like splitting the head of a goat for dinner or serving themselves from the traditional homemade beer barrel. This proverb suggests male pride and a discriminative attitude towards women.

18. *Uhii ni umagwo no uka ndumagwo.*

The boy comes out of childhood, but women never come out of womanhood.[3]

Women will never grow up or change; they will always be women: however, boys grow up to become mature men.

These proverbs are used today to describe women among the Gikuyu people. Other African communities have similar versions and expressions that send the same message demeaning to women. They describe women as inferior, immoral, unpredictable, antisocial, childlike, immature and weak. With all the cultural conditions set to subjugate women as demonstrated above, it is not surprising that female genital mutilation finds a safe haven in such a gender-biased environment. The proverbs are one example of local communication mediums that transmit negative attitudes towards women which directly encourage violence.

False ideologies against women among most African communities have been reinforced for generations through poems, proverbs, oral narratives and traditional songs. Kabira identifies the following attitudes against women by men; they are similar to the ones discussed above:

> *Women should naturally know their place.*
> *Women should accept the "obvious."*
> *Women cannot be thinkers, philosophers, scientists,*
> *   politicians or spiritual leaders.*

Women are homemakers.
Women are to be led, submissive, dependents, mothers.
Women are like earth anyone can sit on.
Women, like the sky, are unpredictable.
Women's natural place is the kitchen.
Women are weak, inferior, and hold babies better.
Women are not ambitious.
Women are by nature mothers.
Women love the noise of children.
A boy grows up to be a man, a woman never grows up.[4]

Socially constructed gender biases and negative attitudes towards women by men become part of male socialization. These biases lay the foundation of objectification, subordination and insensitivity towards women. Gender superiority may also be viewed as a form of cultural blinding that reinforces mistreatment of women. This insensitivity can lead to silence and inaction against female genital mutilation and other forms of violence against women.

Gender bias is evident among other tribes in Kenya, especially with the rituals surrounding the birth of a child. When a baby was born among the Gikuyu people, a boy received five ululations (loud chanting) declaring victory and the arrival of a baby boy. A baby girl received four ululations. The boys were elevated and held with high esteem, but not so for the girls. Boys were showered with gifts of spears, shields, bows, arrows: and leopard skins as symbols of power and status. The message was simple, boys were predestined to become future tribal warriors and leaders, while the girls were shuffled off to the kitchen to learn how to cook and take care of the men just like their mothers. Men labeled women as docile, dependent, foolish, superficial, easy to cheat and of less value than men. These attitudes prevail to this day in many communities around the world. For example, male patients prefer male doctors. In some communities, men doubt and question the professional ability of female doctors. The time has come to systematically dismantle these oppressive, arrogant and violent attitudes toward our very own daughters, sisters and mothers. With these types of attitudes toward women, it is not a surprise that female genital mutilation has been sustained for generations.

There is a myth among the Gikuyu people alive to this day about how men took over and conquered women. According to the myth, women were in power and ruling the entire tribe for generations. The legendary famous female leader was senior chief Wangu wa Makeri. The men could not tolerate her leadership, and they devised a coup de tat. They planned to systematically impregnate their wives, especially those in Senior Chief Wangu's cabinet. During their final stages of pregnancy, when their bodies were physically weak, the men took over the leadership. It happened as planned and the Gikuyu men have lived happily ever after.

Gender biases can indirectly desensitize men, especially in understanding the harmful effects of female genital mutilation and its sustenance. It is sad to notice that some women who carry out the mutilations have internalized and accepted the violence as a norm. It is the worst form of embracing a destructive, damaging act against their very own daughters in the name of culture and tradition. The generational cycle of violence, psychic numbness and tribal loyalty have blinded the perpetrators to the realities of internal trauma and physical pain endured by the victims. There is an urgent need for women to educate women concerning FGM. The suffering innocent victims are our very own sisters, daughters and family members. The communities of faith can do better in providing necessary educational resources encouraging men to join the eradication efforts of all gender based discriminative and abusive practices.

CHIEF WANGU wa MAKERI SENIOR

Weithaga Location, Murang's District
Speculated year of birth: 1865
Speculated year of death: 1936
Picture courtesy of Kenya National Archives, Nairobi

Chapter 2

STORIES OF TERROR AND PAIN

"The oppressed are also God's children, co-creators of history. God does not leave them to perish in the desert without leaving a trace..."

Elsa Tamez

Kenya

In September 1991, a 13-year-old girl bled to death after being mutilated by a "traditional circumciser" in Kitui District, Eastern Kenya. In Kericho District, Western Kenya, 18-year-old Dorothy (not her actual name) bled to death after being circumcised (mutilated) by a "traditional circumciser" at a farmhouse. She bled profusely and died before she could be taken to the nearest health center. Her three co-initiates were treated at the local clinic. In August 1991, Mary (not actual name), also 18 years old, died after being traditionally circumcised by two women in Meru District.[1] The list is endless since majority of the cases are never reported.

Emotions of fear, pain and entrapment as well as imminent death dominate these scenes of violence against innocent girls. The generational cycle of violence is vicious, inhuman and terrorizing. Parents and grandparents perpetuate these indescribably cruel acts against their own daughters simply because every other female in their family has been mutilated and "it is our tradition and culture."

Egypt

Just weeks after Egypt's health minister Ismail Sallam banned circumcision in public hospitals, a 14-year-old girl died after being circumcised at a private hospital in Qualyubiya province, north of Cairo. Security sources said Aisha did not wake up after surgery. The surgeon went into hiding after the operation, and police were investigating any wrongdoing.[2] It is unethical, shameful and disappointing for a professional medical doctor who is supposed to know the damage caused by female genital mutilation to endorse and be a part of a cultural practice that causes harm and, in this case, resulting to death. It is not surprising to find other hospitals in Africa carrying out this practice in secrecy.

According to a medical doctor and a native of Egypt, female genital mutilation is also termed as female sexual castration (FSC) in Egypt. This doctor pioneered a pilot research study on the subject. He blames religious institutions and social customs for the continuation of the practice. He concluded that FGM victims have psychological consequences similar to those of rape victims.[3] The doctor estimates that eight out of every ten Egyptian women have been subjected to female genital mutilation. He recorded statements from victims showing their feelings about genital mutilation:

> *"I was terrified to say no."*
> *"I dare not say no."*
> *"I wasn't fully comprehending what was happening to me."*
> *"I was shocked and never was I able to comprehend until it was over."*
> *"Please don't make me remember what happened; I am trying to forget."*

"I cried and screamed for help, and no one helped."
"I cried like mad, shouting, 'You all cheated me.'" The
    respondent wept silently, then said with a choking
    voice, *"They told me, 'You must be purified like the*
    rest of your sisters.'"
"They attacked me by surprise. I couldn't believe my
    mother was with them; they all attacked me one
    early morning while I was still sleeping."
"I saw the Daya (circumciser) *holding a razor, then she*
    hurt me."[4]

The traumatic impact in these statements is clear: pain, humiliation, torture, hopelessness and shock. They are vivid images and sounds in a torture chamber.

Islam plays a major role in the practice of female sexual castration in Egypt as well as other Islamic communities. The practice known as *sunna* is not a cardinal doctrine mandated by the Holy Quaran and is found in the *Ahadith*, popular sayings of Prophet Muhammad. There is no consensus regarding the legality of FGM among Muslims.

The origins of female genital mutilation in Islamic communities is not certain. In Islam, there are several religious traditions highly suggesting that men have authority over women. This belief sets the conditions for women to be forced into subservient roles, to include practices that expose women to exploitation, violence and oppressive practices like polygamy and discriminative property laws where women can not legally own property.

Islamic religious teachings in reference to female genital mutilation are not directly stated in writing or in oral traditions. One source suggests that social and cultural reasons sustain the practice.[5]

The religious communities have a primary role to play in education, prevention and eradication of female genital mutilation. Consistent long-term educational goals in all institutions of higher learning have great potential in making a difference. Religious instruction should link the eradication of all practices that harm God's creation with other religious doctrines.

Djibouti

The following graphic and gruesome case of female genital mutilation in Djibouti demonstrates the tragic and senseless torture of the innocents:

> *The little girl, entirely nude, is immobilized in the sitting position on a stool by at least three women. One of them with her arms tightly around the little girl's chest; two others hold the child's thighs apart by force, in order to open wide the vulva. The child's arms are tied behind her back, or immobilized by two other women guests. The traditional operator says a short prayer: 'Allah is great and Mohamet (sic) is his prophet. May Allah keep away all evils'. Then she spreads on the floor some offerings to Allah; split maize (corn) or in urban areas, eggs. Then the old woman takes her razor and excises the clitoris.The infibulation follows: the operator cuts with her razor from top to bottom of the small lip and then scrapes the flesh from the inside of the large lip.This nymphectomy and scraping are repeated on the other side of the vulva.The little girl howls and writhes in pain, although strongly held down.*
>
> *...Exhausted, the little girl is then dressed and put in bed. The operation lasts from 15-20 minutes according to the ability of the old woman and the resistance put up by child.*[6]

Violence and abuse in the name of religion is not new to humanity but must be eradicated by all means possible and available to humanity. The story above shows how the innocent victim gives up, accepting her helplessness and powerlessness. She resigns in pain, and unknown permanent psychological and biological damage is done to her young, tender and innocent life.

Sierra Leone

A secret women's society lured 600 refugees in a Sierra Leone camp for displaced people into a mass female genital mutilation ritual. Health workers said that 100 girls, ages 8 to 15, were suffering severe complications. The media reported genital mutilation of a 28-year-old female who was forcibly circumcised by a female cult gang who accused her of spying on the gang. The victim (name withheld) told the Reuters News Service that she was seized at night two months ago by members of the powerful Bondo secret society that defends female circumcision. *"Several of them threw me down on the ground, then they tore my pants and with a blade started slicing."* She needed fifteen stitches and a blood transfusion, according to a gynecologist who treated her and asked not to be identified for her own security.[7]

Sudan

The following was reported verbatim from two Sudanese women:

> *"Long ago my sister died after circumcision. She couldn't pass urine and was not taken to a doctor. One of my daughters, circumcised the pharaonic way, had the same trouble, together with a fever. The doctor did a de-circumcision."*
>
> *"I have been circumcised pharaonically. My daughter, who is 17 now, has not been circumcised. I told her she didn't have to be grateful to me for anything in her life, except that she is uncircumcised'*
>
> —Unnamed married women[8]

It is sad to note that multigenerational tribal and religious bondage in the name of loyalty to our traditions has imprisoned individuals, households and entire tribal regions, both educated and noneducated. This bondage cannot allow them to sense the pain their very own children are experiencing in female genital mutilation. It is encouraging to note the boldness by one of the Sudanese mothers above who stubbornly refused to allow her daughter to face the torture of mutilation. Her own experience of pain may have been a key factor in leading her to take this decisive action.

In Sudan, women who vehemently support the mutilations claim that it promotes cleanliness, increases a girl's chance to find a husband, improves her chances of fertility, protects her virginity and maintains good morals. All these are false cultural and traditional myths. Female genital mutilation exposes the innocent young girl to trauma and other yet-to-be-measured and documented psychological damage.

Togo

A courageous young lady is one of the few immigrants to the United States of America who made the entire world listen to her story of pain and horror as she escaped from being mutilated. She entered the United States illegally and sought refugee status. While she faced double trouble after she was apprehended by the immigration and naturalization service, she continued fighting with the "never give up" African woman warrior spirit. Her asylum was finally granted, but she paid a dear price through her long painful days locked behind bars. Her crime? Running for her dear life. She fled Togo because her tribe demands that all females be mutilated once they are engaged for marriage and a bridal price has been paid to her parents. Forty days after the mutilation, the husband consummates the marriage.[9]

The bold young lady (name withheld) now lives in the United States, having broken free from her bondage. Unfortunately, there are millions of innocent girls, inspired by the African woman warrior spirit, yet they will not be lucky as she was. Someone must hear their cries and respond with haste.

Nigeria

A similar incident happened to a Nigerian woman, (name withheld). At the time of this research, deportation proceedings were ongoing through the immigration and naturalization service. She was in the United States accompanying her husband who was attending college. After the sudden death of her husband, she lost her nonimmigrant visa status. She applied for asylum on the grounds that her then 11-year-old daughter would be subjected to female genital mutilation against her will, if she returned to Nigeria.[10] The outcome of the case was not known by the time this research was completed. I trust that her wishes were granted.

The National Association of Nigeria Nurses and Midwives (NANNM) has been working hard in education and prevention of female genital mutilation. The association identifies FGM as a gender stereotype form of oppression. It is also described as injustice and a violation of human rights deeply rooted in the culture and traditions of the people. The role of religion in fighting the practice should not be overlooked.[11]

The strongly held cultural beliefs can only be dismantled through consistent, long-term commitment to gender education and empowerment. The communities of faith are best positioned to initiate an effective grassroots educational process. Youth groups, young persons of faith organizations, colleges and universities must be involved in the process.

Non-violent marches and public forums will be helpful in creating public awareness and remove the stigma of discussing female genital mutilation in public. New religious education curriculums will need to be inclusive, with a focus on healthy and unhealthy tribal and cultural practices among our people. Cultural blindness that has led to years of servitude and bondage by our sisters must be demolished. The first seeds of change can be planted, nurtured and matured in communities of faith in order to generate change. Standing on the sidelines without action will mean more damaged lives of our very own sisters.

Chapter 3

MISSIONARY EFFORTS GONE WRONG

"Jesus taught his followers in word and deed to consider the gender difference irrelevant to the concerns and to the process of the kingdom of God."

Gilbert Bilezikian

Church Missionary Society

European missionaries introduced Christianity in Kenya. British colonial occupation and colonization efforts marred any good intentions the missionaries had. The local natives always viewed the westerners with suspicion. After all, the missionaries enjoyed security and protection from the colonial forces. Their message was good, but they were guilty by association with their colonial brothers. The Church Missionary Society (CMS), sponsored by the Church of England, found itself deeply engaged with the lives of local natives, including their tribal practices. It was not long before the missionaries faced head-on the practice of female genital mutilation among the Gikuyu community of central Kenya.

The foreign missionaries attempted to understand the ways and customs of the local people, but to this day it is not clear whether they understood the practice of female genital mutilation. The Church Missionary Society and the colonial administrators did not have a consensus on what was the most practical method of responding to female genital mutilation. They did not seem to understand the implications of the actions they were taking while engaging the Gikuyu community in such a deeply rooted tribal belief and cultural practice. The missionaries condemned the practice as "barbaric," just as they did other tribal practices. Condemnation provoked further resistance by the natives, questioning the missionaries' agenda. Missionary interference with tribal practices was met with resistance just as a member of the Gikuyu community, finding himself in downtown London on Christmas Eve, would question the existence of Santa Clause.

Punitive measures were instituted against anyone who allowed their girls to be mutilated. Instead of taking the opportunity to educate the locals, the missionaries locked the gates of their schools and churches to anyone who practiced female genital mutilation. The locked gates of the English churchmen inspired the local natives to establish their own places of worship and schools with renewed energy and opposition against illegal land occupation by the foreigners. Female genital mutilation was just part of the fuel that energized the fires of opposition and resistance against colonial occupation.

One of the English missionaries' outposts was located ten miles north of Nairobi in Kabete. As opposition against female genital mutilation by the missionaries expanded, their colonial brothers were busy stealing and occupying the best parts of land in Kenya. Their actions compounded the problem and the outcome was an established full-scale underground opposition against the foreigners.

The division between the local natives who converted to western Christianity and those who resisted conversion was instant. Colonial administrators maximized and exploited these divisions to solidify their "divide and rule" political ideology. Local opposition gained momentum rallying around female genital mutilation. Needless to say, the CMS efforts in addressing female genital mutilation were ineffective.

The mission council of the Church of Scotland[1] was also active in Central Kenya. The Scottish missionaries used a different approach in addressing female genital mutilation practices. They understood the mutilations as a sacrificial, sanctifying and ritualistic practices. They also understood the practice as female sexual control by men. The mutilation would decrease sexual passion and desire. Less sexual desire meant that the girl's virginity would be preserved until marriage.

Scottish missionaries deserve to be recognized and appreciated for their approach to female genital mutilation, as will be discussed later. To illustrate the weak approach by the CMS leaders, the following is a memorandum of record supporting the banning of female circumcision by one of the English bishops. It exposes the poor approach of the subject by the unnamed bishop:

(i).   *No woman shall perform an operation of circumcision without the sanction and authority of the council.*

(ii). *Every woman thus authorized to perform an operation of circumcision shall be registered in a book kept by the secretary of this council and will be given a written permit authorizing her to perform circumcision operations.*

(iii). *This permit can be withdrawn by this council or by the District Commissioner or by the Assistant District Commissioner.*

(iv). *Any authorized person to perform an operation of circumcision shall not remove more than the clitoris.*

(v).   *Native opinion is not yet sufficiently advanced to render total abolition feasible at present and the resolution is intended simply to limit the operation to the less severe and less harmful form [2].*

This response by the bishop of the church, is weak and compromising from a pastoral care perspective. He advocates for the continuation of female genital mutilation under controlled measures by the colonial government. The bishop demeans the natives and refers to them as not mentally advanced enough to comprehend the importance of discontinuing female genital mutilation. This probably explains why basic education on biological functions of the female genitalia was never considered as a critical educational option by the English missionaries in their struggle against female genital mutilation. After all, how can you teach people whom you have already labeled as not mentally advanced? All human beings are created equal and endowed with God's image. It is not "advanced thinking" to compromise and accept limited forms of female genital mutilation as was the bishop's position. The official response by the church lacks compassion and care for the victims.

A nonjudgmental attitude and unconditional acceptance of the natives by the foreign missioners would have yielded more fruits in their efforts than the compromising legislative approach they seemed to prefer. For example, in one of the CMS outposts in Kahuhia, near Murang'a (then Fort Hall), the British missionaries did not engage the local people from an educational perspective. They used intimidation, expulsions from churches and schools as methods of fighting female genital mutilation. The full-scale resistance by the Gikuyu community should not have come as a surprise to the English clerics.

Church of Scotland Mission

Scottish missionaries understood female genital mutilation, as demonstrated by their approach to conducting systematic education from the medical perspective, and they deserve to be commended. In 1906 Dr. John W. Arthur, a missionary/medical (gynecologist), started his operations in Kikuyu hospital. He joined efforts with Miss M.S. Stevenson, a school teacher (1907-1930) to design a curriculum of instruction for the natives to highlight the dangers of female genital mutilation. Dr. Stanley E. Jones (1914-1924) backed up their efforts by openly campaigning against FGM using education and medical knowledge to show the local people the extent of damage to the female body. For example, the scar tissues hardened the exterior part of the vagina, making it difficult to dilate during labor.[3] The hardening put the child and the mother at a very high risk of losing their lives.

Limited success was achieved, but before long the missionaries started encountering stiff opposition from the local people who saw the church as a branch of the colonial militant oppressors who had occupied their country illegally. The missionaries coached local native female assistants to work as nurses and exposed them to the agony experienced during labor and childbirth as a result of female genital mutilation. The nursing assistants were highly effective in spreading the message about the dangers of FGM to the victims and their families. Unfortunately, it does not appear that this method was highly endorsed to the extent of employing it all over the Gikuyu country. In 1916 there were joint efforts by all the mission groups active in Gikuyu country to ban mutilation, but the chaos of the first world war disrupted their education efforts.

In 1921 the missionaries, possibly out of desperation and frustration, decided that female genital mutilation must be wiped out in their area of operations starting with Githumu, Ng'enda, Kijabe and Kambui. The Rev. W.P. Knapp[4] led the charge, *"Put it out among you or leave the church!"* The first known pamphlets published in the Gikuyu language were distributed in 1923 edited by Dr. Philip and Dr. Jones. Unfortunately, the joint efforts by the missionaries to educate the locals motivated the first organized resistance through the Kikuyu Central Association (KCA), who saw these efforts as further attempts of colonial domination and an attempt to wipe out local customs and traditions by the foreigners.

Political consciousness was rising and the missionaries were viewed with suspicion because they did not condemn the evil actions of the colonialists. How could they speak of a loving God who loved the local African people but still sanction the evil acts of their fellow ruthless colonizers who were occupying native land by force, evicting innocent and defenseless poor? In 1923 Harry Thuku, one of the Gikuyu's great warriors against the British occupying forces, was detained in Kismayu Island because he championed the cause of the poor and their land. Local political activists held land as the number one issue for fighting the white man's illegal and violent occupation. However, since female genital mutilation was one of the heavily emotional issues, the political activists used it to maximize their call against the foreigner's agenda.

The missionaries ordered any church members who did not publicly renounce female genital mutilation to leave. Two hundred members in the Presbyterian Church of Kenya were barred from participating in Holy Communion. This stance only hardened and encouraged the adherents of female genital mutilation to extreme stubbornness and resistance against the missionary message.

The British colonial governor and his administration refused to join the religious groups in their struggle against female genital mutilation. The governor argued that the decision to mutilate or not should be left to individual households. Anti-missionary feelings were running high, as demonstrated by two girls who were in the custody of the missionaries and were forcibly mutilated. The first girl was Ms N, 14, from South Nyeri district; the second one was Ms M, 13, from Kambui; both were severely mutilated.[5]

Missionary intervention compounded the problem of female genital mutilation in the case above. While the missionaries made some gains, overall they lost miserably in building a coherent, practical, non-punitive, educational and liberating means of grace against female genital mutilation in Kenya. The prohibition efforts by the religious groups disengaged and distanced the local people. Did the European missionaries take the time to fully comprehend and systematically understand and address FGM from a solid theological and pastoral care perspective? You, the reader, decide.

The missionary response to FGM underestimated the cultural depth of the practice. Initially, when the medical educational approach from Scotland started out with education without condemnation, it was a great move in the right direction. Use of local nursing assistants to express the damages of mutilation was an excellent and effective move then and can be utilized today. The missionaries failed to persuasively articulate a pastoral, theological and biological approach as to why female genital mutilation was harmful to the young girls.

Punitive measures like denying Holy Communion, school attendance or any other measures by the missionaries was unforgivable. The missionaries also failed to offer pastoral care resources to the innocent victims who had already been mutilated. They were met with rejection and closed doors. The helpless, hurting girls, wounded and hungry for a loving, unconditional acceptance, were abandoned like sheep without a shepherd. What would Jesus do? Love them, embrace them and offer them healing and comfort. The missionaries did some good in Kenya, but in this specific subject they were unsuccessful.

Churches in Kenya Today

The majority of religious communities in Kenya have maintained the status quo and left the issue of female genital mutilation untouched. This slaughter of the innocents continues. The health and welfare of innocent girls and women must be a priority. The voices of prophetesses and prophets must arise and scatter the enemies of liberty and justice for our innocent suffering sisters.

While there are numerous competing priorities for the faith community (HIV-AIDS, poverty, crime, unemployment, corruption), there is no excuse as to why FGM should not be a priority. It is more devastating than all these other social evils in the African Continent today. There is a cultural discomfort when it comes to discussing sexual matters. While the communities of faith should be the moral custodians and are better-positioned to break these cultural barriers, silence seems to be the norm.

Sexuality is part of God's creation and design and is not a shameful subject. An honest and open dialogue about sexual matters must be a priority in all homes and houses of worship, especially among the youth. In the absence of this much-needed information, young people will feed themselves on sexual knowledge from unbalanced and biased sources. Popular media especially movies and popular television shows, glorify sexual immorality and violence against women. An open dialogue with youth in conferences and conventions on female genital mutilation will greatly assist in tearing down the barriers leading to balanced sexual education and eradication of all forms of violence against women.

Chapter 4

PSYCHOLOGICAL MEDICAL AND SEXUAL CONSEQUENCES

"Hope, or its absence in despair, is the basic psycho-spiritual dynamic with which the pastoral caregiver must contend, particularly when attending to a crisis."

Andrew D. Lester

Trauma in Female Genital Mutilation

Female genital mutilation is an internally devastating event in the psyche, leaving behind psychological and emotional wounds. The victim is powerless and overwhelmed by the physical force used by her attackers. The feelings of intense fear, helplessness and loss of control are exhibited by the victim during female genital mutilation. She is literally trapped physically and psychologically. The extreme pain experienced in a mutilation leaves permanent damaging effects on the victim. The mutilation event in Djibouti discussed in Chapter

2 describes the internal woundedness in the victim. Psychological trauma such as experienced in female genital mutilation can be described as a powerful force that causes fear and helplessness on the inside and the threat of death.[1].

The victim is subjected to internalized pain cutting deep into her psyche. This pain leaves a permanent mark in her inner self, well known by the victim.

Another definition of trauma is *"an extraordinary stressor that disrupts normal life routines."*[2]. Trauma may also be compared with a physical wound; however, the wound is internal and permanently sealed in the victim's mind. In female genital mutilation, trauma is an extraordinary stressor that literally includes a physical wound. A similar definition of trauma compared to the above definitions, states that, *"trauma occurs when any act, event or experience harms or damages the physical, sexual, mental, emotional or spiritual integrity of our true self."*[3] Psychological damage resulting from female genital mutilation is immeasurable. Literally, the victim is cut, tearing her flesh and inner self as described in the following explanation of trauma:

> *"Trauma" is an all-purpose term for what we feel when our lives are turned upside down. The Greek root, "traumat-," means "wound," and the connotation of a cut or a bruise or a fracture or a bullet hole provides an apt metaphor...it deals with shocks to the system, lacerations of the spirit, soul damage...Psychological trauma occurs in the wake of an unexpected event that a person has experienced intimately and forcefully.*[4]

With this definition, trauma is present in female genital mutilation. How to measure and assess its impact is another potential research subject. The American Psychological Association (APA) Diagnostic Statistical Manual 4 (DSM-IV is the authoritative reference manual used by therapists, counselors and other caregivers to diagnose psychologically related illnesses). This manual is the standard diagnostic guide in determining and treating various psychological disorders. According to this manual, a person has been exposed to a traumatic event [or events] if both of the following have been present in her or his life:

(1) the person has experienced, witnessed or been confronted with an event that involved actual or threatened death or serious injury, or a threat to the physical integrity of oneself or others (2) the person's response involved intense fear, helplessness, or horror.[5]

The definitions of FGM and the several mutilation events discussed earlier illustrates the helplessness, intense fear and horror of the victim. To describe this as a near-death experience is an understatement. The experiences described in these mutilations fit the clinical definition of trauma above. Further qualitative research will be necessary to scientifically confirm these assumptions.

Long-term psychological evaluation of victims may be able to reveal the nature and extent of trauma experienced by victims of FGM. Further research will be necessary to clinically measure the traumatic levels experienced in female genital mutilation. In cases where the victims of female genital mutilation are old enough to remember the event, it may be easier to conduct interviews and, if possible, long-term therapeutic counseling in a caring relationship.

Documented psychological effects in female genital mutilation are rare in psychological literature. African scholars and caregivers can contribute to quantitative and qualitative research that will confirm current assumptions of multiple psychological consequences in female genital mutilation. DSM-IV records important post traumatic stress disorders (PTSD) that can identify with FGM victims. The World Health Journal reports,

"many psychological problems as a result of circumcision have been reported including anxiety, depression, neuroses, and psychoses."[6]

The 1997 World Health Organization publication details health consequences that will be listed under medical implications below.

The statement highlights psychosexual, psychological and social consequences including trauma.

> *"Almost all types of female genital mutilation involve the removal of part or the whole of the clitoris, which is the main female sexual organ, equivalent in its anatomy and physiology to the male organ, the penis. Sexual dysfunction in both partners may be the result of painful intercourse and reduced sexual sensitivity following clitoridectomy and narrowing of the vaginal opening. The more severe types of FGM, like infibulation, remove larger parts of the genitals, close off the vagina, leaving areas of tough scar tissue in place of sensitive genitals, thus creating permanent damage and dysfunction. FGM may leave a lasting mark on the life and mind of the woman who has undergone it. The psychological complications of FGM may be submerged deeply in the child's subconscious mind, and they may trigger the onset of behavioral disturbances. The possible loss of trust and confidence in those that are the caregivers has been reported as another serious effect. In the longer term, women may suffer feelings of incompleteness, anxiety, depression, chronicity, frigidity, marital conflicts conversion reactions, or even psychosis. Many women traumatized by their FGM may have no acceptable means of expressing their feelings and fears, and suffer in silence. Unfortunately, inadequate research exists to establish scientifically the precise magnitude of psychological and social consequences of FGM, and its effect on child development.*[7]

The understanding of psychological trauma is based on the assumption that female genital mutilation victims exhibit signs that meet the DSM-IV criteria discussed above. The victim is afflicted with extensive physical injury and overwhelmed with intense fear. Horror and hopelessness disrupts and damages her life. Bombardment and brainwashing propaganda that the clitoris or the victim's genitals contain a dirty part, is a "source of irresistible temptations" that needs to be removed, are all falsehoods that must be eliminated.

The violence in the entire mutilation event is unbearable and the damage done unknown:

> *"The fact is that in psychiatric or psychoanalytic terms, we simply do not know what it means to a girl or woman when her central organ of sensory pleasure is cut off, when her lifegiving canal is stitched up amid blood, fear and secrecy, while she is forcibly held down, and told if she screams she will cause the death of her mother, or bring shame on her family."*[8]

A registered mid-wife from Somalia observes that FGM kills self-esteem in mutilated women. She encourages health caregivers to be sensitive to the long-term physical and psychological trauma faced by victims.

> *"Female genital mutilation is a human rights tragedy that represents an extreme example of how societies around the world attempt to suppress women's sexuality, maintain their subjugation, and control their reproductive function. In addition to being illegal, the procedure involves child abuse, torture, and violence against women. Health professionals need to be educated about the history, origins, and practice of female genital mutilation to enable them to support and empower women so that it can be eradicated."*[9]

The medical community can play a major role in educating and counseling women so that they can save their daughters from this damaging experience. Childbirth can be a prime teaching opportunity for mothers. Women can be most effective in disrupting this vicious cycle of violence, especially in communities where women are the majority supporters of FGM and they actually carry out the mutilations themselves.

Human sexuality is an intimate and very personal subject. FGM victims are exposed publicly in overwhelming shame. The victim's shame is repressed and probably comes to the surface if she senses a similar threat that might bring back her painful memories. Repressed memories are held by the victim for a lifetime. Repressed shame must be experienced if we are to come to terms with the good, the bad and the unique of what we are.[10]

Shame might provoke feelings of hopelessness and helplessness and the lack of any desire or energy to speak out against FGM. Encouraging the victims to share their experiences in a safe environment will replace the shame and fear with empowerment. Only the victims can accurately identify their sense of shame, following a near death experience in female genital mutilation. The victim's response is silence as dictated by society. The following explanation of silence in the context of shame might help explain the silence among FGM victims:

> *"Shame is an experience that has not been much talked about in contemporary society, …Shame as Lewis (1987) noted, makes us want to hide; we avert our gaze and hang our head in shame. Shame is so painful that we hope it ends quickly; we have no particular desire to reflect on it or talk about it, because to do so is to run the risk of reexperiencing it. Shame is also somewhat contagious; It is difficult to witness another person's acute shame or embarrassment without some vicarious twinge in ourselves. Exploring others' feelings of shame put us in touch with our own unacknowledged or unmastered shame. We tend to be ashamed of being ashamed and try to deny and hide our shame for that reason."*[11]

The code of silence among tribal societies that practice FGM employs shame to ensure continued silence. If younger siblings ask where their sister has gone during the mutilation season among the Gikuyu people, the response is that she has been "temporary loaned" to her favorite aunt. When the victim returns home, she is welcomed as a hero and cannot violate the code of silence. It is a taboo to speak out openly and publicly about FGM. Silence is the rule, a taboo that cannot be broken. Her feelings of pain and terror are repressed.

A medical doctor from Egypt observed and interviewed over 100 women, victims of completed female genital mutilations. He notes in his study the intense emotional pain marked by weeping, humiliation and shame as the survivors accessed their memories and retold their stories.[12] While the psychological impact has not been documented in a scientific study, one can sense the internal psychological pain and impact in the lives of survivors.

Health Implications

Medical implications reported by the World Health Organization include:

1. *Hemorrhage—severe bleeding, potentially able to cause death or anemia.*

2. *Shock—due to severe pain and anguish; no anesthetic is administered.*

3. *Infections—as a result of unsterilized instruments, crude tools, traditional medicines; and infection may spread to the uterus, fallopian tubes and ovaries.*

4. *Tetanus, septicemia and gangrene all may occur.*

5. *Urine retention—fear of pain on the raw wound (while passing urine) may result in urinary tract infection. Injury to adjacent tissue: when the victim struggles, chances are that other parts in the genitalia get cut, e.g., rectum, vagina and urethra.*

6. *Problems in pregnancy and childbirth—tough tissue scars may prevent dilation.*

7. *The risk of HIV transmission—use of same unsterile crude instruments on all the victims.*[13]

A lecturer in the department of nursing at the University of Southern Queensland, Toowoomba, Australia, demonstrates the role of education during childbirth. She highlights the same views documented earlier, such as the prenatal problems, especially genitourinary infections during pregnancy. She mentions the postpartum period as being traumatic for mutilated women because they relive the birth trauma through reinfibulation, extending the healing time and giving multiple chances of infections. She emphasizes the need for educating health care professionals in the west who are unfamiliar with female genital mutilation practices.

Thousands of emigrant families from Africa where this practice is carried out arrive every month in Europe and North America. Soon or later there will be attempts to carry out some of these traditional practices in their "new homes." While local laws in the west are strict and do forbid this practice, the immigrants are known to have ways of shipping their daughters back to their native lands for a visit, only to be mutilated and shipped back to the west. In Great Britain, according to this study, as many as 2000 girls are mutilated each year through this overseas shipping and return system.[14]

African women of reproductive age have the highest death risk from maternal causes. The *Social Science Journal* states that of all the women ages fifteen to forty-nine living in sub-Saharan Africa, one in twenty-one has a chance of dying of a pregnancy-related cause during her reproductive life.[15]

Africa takes a huge toll with 30 percent of all maternal deaths in the world. There are many factors that contribute to these high numbers, for example: lack of access to health care services, lack of trained birth attendants, obstructed labor, excessive bleeding, severe infection, poor diet for pregnant mothers, unclean water, low cultural status of women (in which case women have no legal rights). Women are in most cases treated like objects, as documented earlier in Chapter 3.

Female genital mutilation also contributes to this high maternal mortality:

"The continuing practice of female circumcision and infibulation in the northern part of sub-Saharan Africa

also contributes to the risks a woman is subjected to during pregnancy and childbirth. Maternal and infant mortality are highest in countries where female circumcision is widely practiced. In some Muslim societies of sub-Saharan Africa, women who are not infibulated are considered prostitutes. Circumcision and infibulation are performed primarily to prevent pre-marital sex. When a woman is married, she must be cut open to allow penetration and more cuts are needed for the delivery of a baby. After the child is born, she is sewn together until the child stops breast-feeding. Then she is once again cut open to allow the resumption of sexual activity.[16]

The violent treatment illustrates the psychological and physical torture women and newly born infants have to endure, ultimately resulting to death for many. A group of medical doctors recently shared the results of a study on female circumcision in the *American Journal of Obstetrics.*[17] The study stated that American obstetrician-gynecologists have had no experience in providing care to women who have been mutilated. A case report details the story of a 36-year-old Sudanese woman who was seen at the University of New Mexico School of Medicine Prenatal clinic at eleven weeks of gestation. She had undergone pharaonic circumcision as a young girl, prior to coming to the United States. She was embarrassed about the vulva scars and in her case she stated that she wanted a female primary-care provider familiar with female circumcision. She also wanted a vaginal birth because she had undergone two caesarian births and had been told by her family that the caesarian births were as a result of her "moral weakness."

According to the medical team, performing an adequate pelvic examination was almost impossible due to the vulva scarring that occurred when she underwent female genital mutilation. At thirty-nine weeks gestation, she had further complications and was admitted to labor and delivery. To place a foley catheter was difficult because the meatus was obscured by vulva scar tissue. Epidural anesthesia was administered and the patient's pain eased. Further examination revealed that she was missing the external genitalia;

namely the labia minora, clitoral area and the external urinary meatus had been damaged. Successful vaginal birth occurred after nineteen hours of labor, and the patient was discharged from the hospital with a healthy baby boy after two days.

The effects of female genital mutilation clearly put her and the infant at a very high risk. Were it not for a highly advanced medical facility and a willing medical team, the results could have been fatal. The doctors noted that emotional trauma does occur during female genital mutilation, given the magnitude of the scars they had to deal with as illustrated in their patient above. The side effects during birth can be devastating:

> *"The gynecologic problems include keloid formation, vulva dermal inclusion cysts, recurrent urinary tract infection, dysmenorrhea, hematocolpos, dysparenuia, recurrent vaginitis, chronic pelvic infection, pelvic pain, and infertility. The major obstetric problem is prolongation of the second stage of labor because of scar tissue dystocia, with the attendant need for "anterior episiotomy" (deinfibulation). Vesicovaginal and rectovaginal fistulas, laceration of the scar tissue with subsequent hemorrhage, and fetal asphyxia or death are common sequelae in women who labor unattended with an obstructed introitus. Additionally, infibulation makes vaginal examination in labor very difficult and painful, resulting in the inability to effectively monitor the progress of labor.*[18]

The above account provides scientific documentation of the consequences noted earlier from the World Health Organization report. The medical community in Africa has a major responsibility and must be aggressive in counseling and educating women against female genital mutilation. However, even among the elite in the medical community, it is not a surprise to find some who may be supportive of female genital mutilation. An interdisciplinary approach with medical practitioners, clergy, college professors, students and ordinary people from the villages in Africa can be highly effective in teaching the effects of female genital mutilation. Clergy and the medical community must act urgently in leading an open public dialogue about this harmful practice. It will literally take the whole village to raise the girl child.

An article in the East African Medical Journal stated the following consequences:

"The medical complications of the practice of circumcision were studied in 290 Somali women between ages of 18-54. Thirty-nine percent of the interviewed women had experienced significant complications after circumcision, most commonly hemorrhage, infection or urinary retention. Thirty-seven of the women reported a late complication of circumcision. Among these complications were dermoid cyst at the site of the amputated clitoris, urinary problems such as pain at micturition, dribbling urine incontinence and poor urinary flow. Forty of the women had experienced problems at the time of menarche and ten of them were operated on because of haematocolpos. Most of the married women of the study sample were deinfibulated naturally by their husbands.[19]

This illustration provides another scientific documentation confirming the consequences faced by victims of female genital mutilation. The *American Journal of Nursing,* supports the above findings. An Australian health professional, who is a registered nurse and a community health lecturer at the University of Arizona College of Nursing, describes her interviews with eleven mutilated women attending the college. The highlights of her interview illustrated trauma and fear as a result of their experiences.[20]

The women were from Sudan, Somalia and Egypt. All except two had given birth to children in the United States. The most fear among these survivors was revisited during childbirth in cases where reinfibulation must occur. The eleven women stated that they had experienced painful pelvic examinations. The report also states that mutilated women are extremely fearful of the first sexual contact with a male in cases where the woman has been infibulated.

Now the man has the task of forcibly opening her up with a sharp instrument, or fingernail grown for that purpose. The immediate result in such cases includes, painful intercourse, perineal lacerations, infections and hemorrhage.

The role of education in eradicating female genital mutilation by the medical community cannot be overemphasized. In Sudan, the following was observed:

> *"Among the more educated members of the male Sudanese society and particularly the young educated male, there is a strong attitude against the practice of infibulation, clitoridectomy or any other excision of female external genitalia. ...eventually spoil one of man's and woman's most joyful pursuits: giving one another physical and emotional pleasure through the act of sexual love."*[21]

There seems to be a gleam of hope from the Sudanese community. Publicity and media campaigns sharing the community's feelings and opposition against female genital mutilation will be the beginning of an entire new generation that will value, honor and treat women with integrity and respect.

Sexual Functioning

Few clinical studies have been conducted to show the effects of female genital mutilation and sexual functioning. One medical observation states that mutilation affects sexual functioning and calls for further research.[22]

Female and male sexual functioning should be one of the primary subjects during premarital counseling, and the communities of faith have the moral responsibility and obligation to offer this much-needed education. There is a false assumption that public school teachers are responsible for teaching sex education. This is an area where parents, teachers and religious communities must join hands and offer a factual, balanced and morality-based teaching on sexuality.

A recent article in one of the leading newspapers in Kenya, *The Daily Nation*, carried a story of a 24-year-old female missionary and a local Kenyan man. The man defended female genital mutilation on the grounds of culture and tradition. The female missionary highlighted basic biological factors regarding the female genitalia and showed how this affects sexual pleasure. Effective sexual functioning in female anatomy includes orgasm that is achieved during lovemaking in the God- designed context of marriage. She further clarified that God created both male and female with the capacity to reach orgasm during intercourse for mutual satisfaction.[23]

Cutting off the clitoris reduces a woman's ability to experience sexual pleasure in its fullness. Eradicating female genital mutilation will benefit both men and women in bringing total fulfillment during the sexual act, as God intended it to be in the marriage union. Education on the basic biological functioning of the clitoris during sexual intercourse will eliminate the ignorance surrounding the female genitalia. Lovemaking must focus on mutual satisfaction of both husband and wife. Female genital mutilation in reference to female sexual functioning must be seen as a form of severe limitation that deprives and weakens a couple's love life.

The subject of FGM cannot be discussed without a sincere look at female sexual satisfaction. Experiences of women must be listened and attended to. At Simmons College in Boston, Massachusetts, one of the instructors articulates the difficulties of conducting research on female sexuality as follows:

(i). *It is an area of intimate functioning that poses practical and ethical obstacles to objective research.*

(ii). *There have been careless definitions of terms. Vaginal and clitoral orgasms have been poorly defined, and it is often unclear whether areas of stimulation or areas of experience are being discussed.*

(iii). *Women experience many different patterns of sexuality.*

(iv). *Female sexuality has become a feminist political issue'.* [24]

Regardless of all the above challenges to research in this field, women and men must willingly address the mutilation crisis in Africa. This chapter attempted to show that female genital mutilation causes psychological trauma and other permanent biological damages in the lives of women. It also illustrated from a medical perspective the fact that the birthing process for women may mean death due to FGM related complications. The victims are forced to relive the pain of the mutilation trauma all over again when giving birth, especially in cases where they have been infibulated and must face reinfibulation. Available medical and psychological data shows no benefits in carrying out this practice.

The American Medical News (AMA) identifies female genital mutilation as a *"dangerous, deadly, physically and psychologically scarring procedure … 'We as humanitarians and particularly as gynecologists cannot allow females or any group of patients to be mutilated. I'm afraid that this is even more basic than religion. This is humanitarian.'*[25] A strong foundation from the medical perspective needs to be the way forward toward eradication efforts through aggressive education awareness campaigns.

AIDS-HIV Risks

A life-threatening danger facing victims of female genital mutilation is the very high risk of other infectious diseases transmitted through the shared crude instruments (razor blades, knives, needles) during mutilation. These tools are unsterilized and blood is transmitted from one victim to another during mutilation. While there are various ways in which HIV is transmitted, the most common ones include sexual intercourse, injection of blood, mother-child relationship through breast milk or placenta. While sexual contact remains the most dangerous form of exposure in Africa today, genital mutilation no doubt is a guaranteed method of spreading the HIV virus.

The dual message is clear: stop having sex with multiple partners or die! Stop cutting innocent girls with crude razor blades and knives that have a very high chance of being contaminated with the

HIV virus. If the infections or excessive bleeding do not kill the victims, HIV-AIDS will. HIV is the virus that causes AIDS. HIV can be found in the shared knives, razor blades and even hands of the cruel circumcisers. As for those who have been victimized twice through female genital mutilation and exposure to AIDS, the pain of those affected by these losses is unbearable. These are our very own innocent and defenseless sisters; can we afford to watch on the sidelines?

The community of faith must remind her members that AIDS is not a punishment from God. People with AIDS must not be treated differently. People with AIDS must not be discriminated against, regardless of how they got the virus. They need our love, unconditional acceptance and support. Touching their lives with compassion, sharing hope and helping them face one day at a time and bringing them closer to God is our mission.

The medical community must aggressively address the dangers of using the crude tools circumcisers use to cut innocent girls. If they are not stopped, they simply become agents of death and destruction to young, innocent lives in the name of culture and tradition. More research and education resources are necessary in this particular area, and the medical community can be proactive and help in this war against female genital mutilation with the HIV-AIDS connection. The Kenyan government declared AIDS as a national disaster, a step in the right direction. But will the traditional circumcisers wake up from their cultural slumber and get the message? Whatever choice they will make, it will mean life or death to an innocent unsuspecting girl child.

Chapter 5

PASTORAL CARE BIBLICAL CONSIDERATIONS AND CULTURE

"Moments of failed ministry with women occur when a pastor simply does not understand what to say or do for a parishioner. Good intentions are not sufficient for helpful presence."

Maxine Glaz and Jeann Stevenson Moessner

Victims of traumatic abusive events need empowerment to help them on their journey to wellness.[1] Survivors of female genital mutilation have very personal stories of pain, hopelessness, courage and faith that must be heard. Pastoral caregivers must seek opportunities to minister grace and healing to the victims. Spiritual openness in order to discern God's wisdom during the intervention needs to be part of the delicate approach in pastoral care. Empathetic and nonjudgmental listening will empower the survivors as they struggle toward healing and wellness. The following considerations for pastoral caregivers are offered for further reflection:

(i). Be available to listen and hear the survivor's experienced grief. Allow yourself to come alongside and feel with the victim. Immersing oneself in her pain will make the connection that empowers her to recover her life [2] once again.

(ii). Name female genital mutilation as a violent extreme form of sexual abuse.

(iii). Seek justice for survivors and punishment for the perpetrators.

(iv). Accept community responsibility to stop female genital mutilation.

(v). Enact and enforce legislation against those who subject girls to genital mutilation.

A pastoral care approach that pays attention to the pain of the survivor will enable and empower the victim to talk about her pain. Being able to tune in and listen to her pain and share her feelings can break down the barriers between the pastoral caregiver and the survivor. Given the secrecy and shame that surrounds female genital mutilation, the pastoral caregiver must be extremely sensitive and patient with the survivor and avoid imposing herself or himself by asking irrelevant and unnecessary questions. The victim has the power to disclose what she feels will meet her needs without being pressurized for unnecessary details.

The primary job for the caregiver is to be fully present, engaged, giving her undivided attention. Attending to the internal feelings as they are unveiled, be a presence that communicates God's unconditional love, care and compassion. That sacred moment can be transforming, enabling the victim to move toward feeling understood and empowered. The victim will be empowered to feel like a person again with integrity and a second chance to recover and join the community as a valued member, especially within the community of faith. [3]

A caring pastoral response to survivors of female genital mutilation is critical to the recovery process. The community of faith should be proactive in her prevention efforts through unconditional acceptance and understanding. To break the cycle of silence, a pastoral and theological intervention by the communities of faith is necessary. Breaking the cycle of silence within the community of faith will encourage the victim and the society at large to do likewise, and in the end, all these cycles of shame and violence will be dismantled. [4]

Commitment to pastoral care for the survivors and education to potential victims and perpetrators will make headway in stopping sexual violence against women. The religious communities cannot afford silence at the expense of their members. For example, in Kenya, 80 percent of the population claims to be Christian. The Bible has been translated into local dialects and is read and taught for the most part in schools and churches. Pastoral care from a biblical perspective can change the understanding of female genital mutilation and other violent acts against women. The religious environment can provide safe and trusting relationships where victims find hope and faith to live by. Education and empowerment processes should include biblical teachings and their relationship to culture.

Definition of Culture from Christian Perspective

Culture may be defined as a way of life, behavior, practices that govern a people's lifestyle, diet, taboos, dress, and other patterned ways of living. The definition may also include rites of passage, namely birth, initiation, marriage, adulthood and death with rituals surrounding each of these events. Culture is not evil at all; however, specific practices must be closely examined in the light of the Christian faith. What does embracing the good news, the Gospel, require of those who commit themselves to follow Jesus Christ as the Lord of all aspects of their living? Accepting Jesus Christ means that one has fully embraced the authority of the living Word of God. Some specific cultural practices are in direct violation of biblical teachings.

The Christian person must reject all these practices without any exceptions. There are various cultural expressions in Africa that are unique, valuable and worthwhile to preserve. There are openly known inhuman and abusive practices in the name of cultural heritage and identity that have no place in our lives today. Such must be rejected. If the Christian person truly subjects himself and herself under the authority of the Word of God, the first priority will be to walk in obedience to God's Word and not cultural and tribal requirements.

Accepting biblical authority will lead to spiritual freedom from harmful cultural practices like female genital mutilation, spouse and child abuse. These are fundamental wrongs across humanity and African Christians are no different. Rejecting these harmful cultural practices is an admission that human beings share basic fundamental paradigms not limited to any culture or tribe. It is also an admission that certain cultural practices have no spiritual, social or cultural value. All abusive practices in the light of God's Word must be eliminated.

What Purpose Does Culture Serve?

Culture serves the purpose of identity and helps explain one's family of origin. Certain Cultural practices enrich and inform who we are as God's children, created in God's own image but expressed in a variety of different ethnic and racial ways. For example, the ability to speak different languages, variety of dress, diet, naming of children—all these and many others are not evil. God gave human beings a variety of identities and different ways of expressing ourselves in life.

As limited and sinful human beings, we have added to what God gave us, creating havoc among our fellow human beings. The additional practices outside God's divine purpose are dangerous, harmful and ungodly. Any cultural or tribal practice that causes other human beings to suffer is not from God and must be eliminated.

In addressing female genital mutilation, it is important to understand that no one can truthfully trace the origin of this practice. As a believer, however, the sinful human condition would be the first suspect. The argument that this practice enhances maturity, marriage, and is a rite of passage is just an excuse to abuse, torture and traumatize innocent and helpless girls. What purpose does mutilating girls serve? What exactly is the intended outcome of such a horrible practice? What is symbolic and of tribal value to warrant such a painful practice that has in some instances results in death?

While those advocating for this practice will fight to the hilt defending what they believe to be a real felt need, the Christian person must stand and choose to walk in obedience to God's Word. Subjecting every cultural practice to the biblical test will greatly help in determining what cultural practices need to go and which ones should stay. The authority of Scripture and a genuine conversion to the Christian faith, the leading of the Holy Spirit will assist us in determining the will of God for our lives as African Christians.

Until there is a clear understanding and a genuine heartfelt conversion and transformation, it will be easy to wear the label Christian without bearing any fruits. Female genital mutilation is a deeply rooted belief and eliminating it will take more than a conversion experience. It will take education, discernment and total surrender to the Word of God. It will take spiritual liberation and living in obedience to the Word of God.

Biblical Authority and Culture

The authority of the Bible is rooted in the belief that God inspired human beings by the power of the Holy Spirit to write a living document that permanently transforms cultural beliefs and practices of all those who believe and obey the written Word of God. The Holy Spirit acted directly in transmitting Scripture through human beings and hence all cultural beliefs and practices must be weighed and evaluated through the living Word of God. God spoke through the writers and what they wrote long ago has direct impact in our lives as believers today. In the Word, God speaks and guides us. In the Word, Jesus Christ became human and lived as we do to demonstrate and pattern obedience for the believer. In the Word, we find the standard to measure against all cultural and tribal practices. In obedience to the Word of God as African Christians we accept the Holy Spirit to rule and guide our lifestyle. Our entire outlook of life is based on living in obedience to God.

Without any reservations, we must allow the Holy Spirit to illuminate our hearts and minds to let go of all the cultural practices that are contrary to the written Word of God. Discerning the authority of Scripture and living in obedience will enable us to live out biblical teachings to the best of our ability. This kind of living will produce the internal transformation that can only come about through the power of the Holy Spirit to break free from these deeply held African cultural and tribal beliefs and practices that seem so difficult to break free from.

While the Word of God was written and revealed within a specific cultural setting in the Middle East, in a variety of languages, the task of in-depth study is required today. In order for us to apply these teachings in our lives today, we must be able to inwardly digest them for these teachings to produce the desired outcome of obedience in daily living. By the grace of God, the Scriptures have been translated into many local African languages and dialects. These translations enable and aid the interpretation process of Scripture which in turn assists in understanding and digesting the truths of Scripture, producing spiritual growth and maturity in the believer. Our cultural beliefs and practices as African Christians must be secondary to our faith in Jesus Christ. In Acts 5:29 the apostles found themselves in direct conflict with the Sanhedrin. They were accused by the Sadducees of speaking and healing in the name of Jesus Christ. When they were brought before the convened court, Peter gave a strong witness: *Peter and the other apostles replied: "we must obey God rather than men."* Risk-taking in the defense of the truths of the Gospel is not new, and the African

Church leaders must demonstrate the same level of obedience, courage and loyalty to God and his Word.

Jesus, in addressing the question of clean and unclean ceremonial and cultural practice among the Pharisees challenged them to a higher standard in Mark 7:8,9. *"You have let go of the commands of God and are holding on to the traditions of men."* And he said to them: *"You have a fine way of setting aside the commands of God in order to observe your own traditions."* Paul sounded the same warning to the Colossian brethren, Colossians 2:8. *"See to it that no one takes you captive through hollow and deceptive philosophy, which depends on human tradition and the basic principles of this world rather than on Christ."*

Paul, writing to Titus, warned of myths that might contradict or confuse his faith and standing in Christ, Titus 1:13-16, *"This testimony is true. Therefore, rebuke them sharply, so that they will be sound in the faith and will pay no attention to Jewish myths or to commands, of those who reject the truth. To the pure, all things are pure, but to those who are corrupted and do not believe, nothing is pure. In fact, both their minds and consciences are corrupted. They claim to know God, but by their actions they deny him. They are detestable, disobedient and unfit for doing anything good."*

Full acceptance of biblical authority and the Lordship of Jesus Christ as Savior and Redeemer of all will lead us closer to obedient living. The Word of God will have maximum impact in our lives. With the above discussion on culture and biblical authority, I invite you to reflect further on the following biblical stories of pain, hope and courage in the lives of several biblical women. The church leaders in Africa can no longer afford to ignore the harmful, inhuman and sinful cultural practices surrounding our houses of worship. Domestic violence, child abuse and female genital mutilation are just a few of these destructive cultural practices that must be addressed and eliminated. God is counting on you to do something about it.

Biblical Stories of Pain, Hope and Courage

The Bible does not legitimize violence against women and innocent children, nor does it advocate silence or compromise. The Bible offers a powerful basis for dialogue and practical lessons against violence towards women. Pastoral education with the hope of eradicating female genital mutilation will require biblical teachings with practical application to daily living.

In Kenya and other African countries today, there is an urgent need to restate with clarity the place of women in the church and in the home as taught in the Scriptures. Scriptural teachings do not advocate subservient roles for women as sometimes expressed by various communities of faith who object to spiritual and religious leadership by women. The majority of women and some men who are ardent supporters of FGM also claim their belief in God and believe that the Bible is the Word of God that speaks to their human condition today. However, there seem to be significant gaps and selective understanding and application of biblical truths. It is not uncommon for some pastors and church elders to physically and violently abuse their spouses. The darkness of silence in these cases is shocking. These abusive Christians must be exposed and their works of darkness. Holistic and practical education will pay great dividends.[5]

There is power in the grace of God to break open the stubborn hearts of women and men supporters of FGM. Using specific stories from the Bible, several themes will be highlighted to show that God identifies with the pain and violent treatment against innocent girls and women. There is no gender discrimination or preference from God's point of view. *"Femaleness pertains to the image of God as fully as maleness. God is neither male nor female. He (sic) transcends both genders since they are both comprehended within his being."*[6]

Women are fearfully and wonderfully made, complete and whole, with no deficiencies that need to be corrected. This slaughter of the innocents must stop. Men must join hands with their sisters in affliction and together fight for freedom from tribal and cultural sexual violence expressed in FGM.

Eve (life)

> *Then God said, "Let us make man in our image, in our*
> *likeness, and let them rule over the fish of the sea and the*
> *birds of the air, over the livestock, over all the earth, and*
> *over all the creatures that move along the ground." So*
> *God created man in his own image, in the image of God*
> *he created him; male and female he created them.*
>
> Genesis 1:26-27

In God's own image, women and men were created. There was no hierarchy or gender preferential order, in God's image women and men were created. There was no special, elevated place for men from the beginning of time. The image of God proposition articulates the relational and equal aspects of both male and female at creation. Mutuality in relationship was God's idea at creation for both women and men. They are equally redeemed by the same grace of God. They are both gifted, talented, anointed, called and sent out to serve God on an equal basis; mutual and equal relationship was God's idea.[8]

The departure from the original order of creation occurred at the fall of the first family, Adam and Eve. Accepting the original divine design for humankind will facilitate healing and restoration between men and women. This text should erase any doubts as to what was God's original order at creation.

Full acceptance of women in the church, acknowledging their voice and paying attention to their concerns, will be the way forward. Eve was tempted and Adam seconded her actions, but she was later victorious to the extent that in her old age God blessed the first family with a son, Seth from whom the ancestry of Jesus Christ is found. She was not only the mother of all humankind but also one through whom the Savior of all humankind was later born. Thanks be to God for all women and mothers. They have a central place in God's plan and in our houses of worship and community at large. Acceptance and affirmation will strengthen and encourage our sisters to effectively address domestic, social and cultural violence.

Dinah

Now Dinah the daughter of Leah, whom she had borne to Jacob went out to visit the women of the region. When Shechem son of Hamor the Hivite, prince of the region, saw her, he seized her and lay with her by force. And his soul was drawn to Dinah daughter of Jacob; he loved the girl, *and spoke tenderly to her. So Shechem spoke to his father Hamor, saying, "Get me this girl to be my wife." Now Jacob heard that Shechem had defiled his daughter Dinah; but his sons were with his cattle in the field, so Jacob held his peace until they came...The sons of Jacob answered Shechem and his father Hamor deceitfully, because he had defiled their sister Dinah. They said to them, "We cannot do this thing, to give our sister to one who is not circumcised, for that would be a disgrace to us. Only on this condition will we consent to you: that you will become as we are and every male among you be circumcised. Then we will give our daughters to you and we will take your daughters for ourselves, and we will live among you and become one people"...and every male was circumcised,...on the third day, when they were still in pain, two of the sons of Jacob, Simeon and Levi, Dinah's brothers took their swords and came against the city unawares and killed all males...*

Genesis 34:1-5, 13-16, 25

How would Dinah tell her story of trauma, pain and betrayal? Rape is implied in the original translation. This is a deeply troubling story. Dinah's immediate family administered justice to the perpetrators on behalf of their sister. Survivors of female genital mutilation, rape, domestic violence can identify with Dinah's pain. "Justice be our shield and defender," is a phrase in the Kenyan national anthem, but unfortunately justice has never been the shield and defender for innocent victims of female genital mutilation.

Like Dinah, FGM victims have rights and cannot be ignored or pushed aside:

Pastoral care education for survivors of female genital mutilation must address justice and the needs of the individual. The empowering process must include opportunities for storytelling from the survivor's perspective. Her voice must be heard. Her voice must be allowed to pierce and stir up the conscience of the perpetrators as well as those who stood by the side, heard the cries of the helpless victims and did nothing. From every community of faith, in villages and urban areas, these stories must be told over and over again. May the intervention built on life experiences of pain and torture provoke a deep sense of shame and regret among those who have watched helpless girls suffer and done nothing. Such actions might plant the seeds of indignation and a desire to eliminate this evil and heinous crime against women that has lived among us for centuries.

Unnamed Concubine from Bethlehem

While they were enjoying themselves, the men of the city, a perverse lot, surrounded the house, and started pounding on the door. They said to the old man, the master of the house, "Bring out the man who came into your house, so that we may have intercourse with him". And the man, the master of the house, went out to them and said to them, "No my brothers, do not act so wickedly. Since this man is my guest, do not do this vile thing. Here are my virgin daughter and his concubine; let me bring them out now. Ravish them and do whatever you want to them; but against this man do not do such a vile thing." But the men would not listen to him. So the man seized his concubine, and put her out to them. They wantonly raped her, and abused her all through the night until the morning. And as dawn began to break, they let her go...In the morning her master got up, opened the doors of the house, and when he went out to go on his way, there was his concubine lying at the door of the house, with her hands on the threshold. "Get up", he said to her, "We are going". But there was no answer. Then he put her on the donkey; and the man set out for his home. When he had entered his house, he took a knife, and grasping his concubine he cut her into twelve pieces, limb by limb, and sent her throughout all the territory of Israel. NRSV

Judges 19:22-29

The story is extremely gross and very troubling. The men in the story give up the innocent, defenseless and helpless woman to be raped and tortured. The unnamed concubine who had escaped from the hands of his abuser dies on her way back to the same abusive environment. Who can read this story and fail to identify with the victim? Who can listen to stories of innocent young girls of torture, violence and abuse and fail to empathize with them?

Their cries for justice go unheeded. Survivors of female genital mutilation can identify with the victims in this story. Where and when will justice be administered? More questions are raised by this story than answers. The story demonstrates the suffering of an innocent woman as silent onlookers ignored her need for safety and security, a fitting scenario for FGM. While the majority of perpetrators are women, the shocking silence of men is not excusable. Silence suggests endorsement. One commentator had the following to say about this story, *"to keep quiet is to sin... the story is alive, and all is not well. Beyond confession we must take counsel to say, 'Never again'"*[11]

The call to repentance is divine. All pastors and ministers of religion who speak in the name of God must confess that they have sinned. They have committed the sin of omission through their silence, failed their sisters and fellow humans. Silence in the midst of such an extent of torture, death and destruction in female genital mutilation compromises and weakens our claims of faith and spiritual liberation in Jesus Christ. The call is urgent: stop! Turn around and defend our innocent and helpless sisters who cry daily for help. Evil thrives in silence. The only reason suffering will continue among our innocent sisters is simply because our communities of faith have chosen to look away and assume all is well. No, all is not well! It is time to rise up and vow, "Never again." Now is the time of opportunity and you are the voice.

Tamar

Some time passed. David's son Absalom had a beautiful sister whose name was Tamar; and David's son Amnon fell in love with her. Amnon was so tormented that he made himself ill because of his sister Tamar, for she was a virgin and it seemed impossible to Amnon to do anything to her. But Amnon had a friend whose name was Jonadab the son of David's brother Shimeah; and Jonadab was a very crafty man. He said to him, "O son of the King, why are you so haggard morning after morning? Will you not tell me? Amnon said to him, "I love Tamar, my brother Absalom's sister." Jonadab said to him, "Lie down on your bed, and pretend to be ill; and when your father comes to see you, say to him, "let my sister Tamar come and give me something to eat, and prepare the food in my sight, so that I may see it and eat it from her hand". So Amnon lay down and pretended to be ill; then Amnon said to Tamar, "Bring the food into the chamber to Amnon ….But when she brought them near him to eat, he took hold of her, and said to her, "Come, lie with me, my sister". She answered him, "No, my brother, do not force me; for such a thing is not done in Israel; do not do anything so vile! As for me where could I carry my shame? And as for you, you would be as one of the scoundrels in Israel. Now therefore, I beg you, speak to the King; for he will not withhold me from you"…but he would not listen to her; and being stronger than she, he forced her and lay with her. Then Amnon was seized with a great loathing for her; indeed his loathing was even greater than the lust he felt for her. Amnon said to her, "Get out!" but she said, "No, my brother, for this wrong in sending me away is greater than the other you did to me". But he would not listen to her. He called the young man who served him and said, "Put this woman out of my presence, and bolt the door after her"…She put her hand on her head and she went away crying aloud as she went.

Her brother Absalom said to her, "Has Amnon your brother been with you? Be quiet for now, my sister; he is your brother; do not take this to heart". So Tamar remained a desolate woman, in her brother Absalom's house. When King David heard of all these things, he became angry but he would not punish his son Amnon because he loved him for he was his firstborn, NRSV

2 Samuel 13:1-7, 10-21

This story is horrific and painful. Tamar, daughter of David and Michal, an innocent young girl falls under the hands of two evil trickery men. She was violently and helplessly raped by Amnon, her half brother, despite her cries of appeal and reason:

"No, my brother"
"Do not force me"
"Do not do anything vile"
"As for me, where could I carry my shame?"
"No, my brother, for this is wrong in sending me away..."
"Tamar remained a desolate woman"

The cries of the victim, her resistance, her sound common sense in a moment of crisis go unheaded. The beast of a man, Amnon, possessed with the demon of lust and instant sexual gratification, violated a helpless, innocent girl. He brutally raped Tamar and kicked her out of his house. The words used here by Amnon resemble very much the words used by Sarah when she ordered Abraham to kick Hagar out of their household. Listen to Amnon's words: *"Put this woman out of my presence, and bolt the door after her."* This is what Sarah said: *"Cast out this slave woman with her son"...so Abraham rose early in the morning, and took bread and a skin of water, and gave it to Hagar, putting it on her shoulder, along with the child, and sent her away, NRSV* (Gen. 21:10,14). Rejection is a joint theme shared by these two stories. Even the *"man after God's own heart,"* David, who had experienced rejection and near death experiences in the hands of his enemies does not seem to have been alarmed by the evil his son had committed. On the contrary,

David is said to have responded indifferently because he *"loved him and he was his first born son."* Is the male child more valuable than the female and thus deserving of preferential treatment? Why does the poor innocent girl Tamar, in David's assessment, deserve neglect?

David's stance is deeply troubling. His failure to administer justice provoked his other son Absalom, Tamar's full brother, to give Amnon a taste of justice and he had him killed. The community of faith must wake up from her slumber, take immediate steps to repent of the sinful and ungodly treatment women have continued to suffer. May God stir up Absalom-like faith, boldness and spiritual strength to join hands in eliminating the female genital mutilation menace in Africa.

Deborah

Deborah, a prophetess, the wife of Lappidoth, was leading Israel at that time. She held court under the Palm of Deborah between Ramah and Bethel in the hill country of Ephraim, and the Israelites came to her to have their disputes decided.

Judges 4:4-5

Deborah was a God-appointed chief executive officer, deliverer of the nation of Israel. Sisera was the enemy ruler with iron chariots that he terrorized Israel with. God used Deborah to prophesy that the enemies would soon be defeated. She sent for Barak and gave him the message that God was going to grant them victory over their twenty years of enemy occupation and terror. Barak agreed to undertake the mission by faith, but with one other condition; he wanted Deborah to accompany the soldiers to the battlefield, and she did. God sent a storm that caused the enemy chariots to get stuck in the mud. The foot soldiers pursued and exterminated the enemy. Judges 5 details the song of Deborah, praising God for granting them victory over their enemies. May the Lord raise more Deborahs to do exploits for God in Africa today. This story (Judg. 4-5) speaks and stands by itself as to what God has done in the past, present and future using our sisters. They have a place at the table. Called, anointed and sent by God, just as men are.

Bathsheba

One evening David got up from his bed and walked around on the roof of the palace. From the roof he saw a woman bathing. The woman was very beautiful, and David sent someone to find out about her. The man said, "Isn't this Bathsheba, the daughter of Eliam and the wife of Uriah the Hittite?" Then David sent messengers to get her. She came to him, and he slept with her. (She had purified herself from her uncleanness) Then she went back home. The woman conceived and sent word to David, saying, "I am pregnant."

2 Samuel 11:2-5

David did not score very high points with the way he treated women. Earlier, it was noted how he ignored his own daughter who had been brutally raped by a family member (2 Sam. 13). He only became angry with Amnon, the perpetrator, but could not punish him. This time round he strikes unsuspecting woman. He watched her bathing, lusted for her, sent for her, ordered her in bed, impregnated her and had her husband killed in the battlefield to cover his tracks.

God intervened and executed justice through Prophet Nathan and David repented of his evil (Ps. 50,51), but Bathsheba had to bear the shame, the burden of loosing her life, her marriage, her husband, her newly born child and forcible marriage to King David. Later, God prospered her and she became the mother of the wisest man ever to rule in Israel and the world, Solomon. How could she tell her story of pain and terror today? Bathsheba will forever remain as an inspiration to all women living in communities of oppression. Noble, spiritually strong, an intelligent woman who did not quit during the darkest days of her life. There is hope for victims of gender discrimination, exploitation and all other forms of oppression.

The message of Jesus Christ to suffering women living in communities of oppression was religiously and culturally straightforward;

all matters of gender were irrelevant in relation to true discipleship, access to God, the grace and mercies of God. Women were fully accepted as members of the faith community. Jesus Christ did not exclude women in his ministry. Rather than engaging in religious debates about the place of women, he demonstrated what their place would be: at his feet listening to his teachings and on the road traveling with him as witnesses of the good news of repentance and salvation. Jesus Christ invited and participated with women in ministry as recorded in the New Testament, tearing down the barriers of gender and religious discrimination against women. The following stories illustrate the inclusive ministry of Jesus Christ as a model for us to follow today:

Mary, Mother of Jesus

This is how the birth of Jesus Christ came about. His mother Mary was pledged to be married to Joseph, but before they came together, she was found to be with child through the Holy Spirit. Because Joseph her husband was a righteous man and did not want to expose her to public disgrace, he had in mind to divorce her quietly. But after he had considered this, an angel of the Lord appeared to him in a dream and said, "Joseph son of David, do not be afraid to take Mary home as your wife, because what is conceived in her is from the Holy Spirit. She will give birth to a son, and you are to give him the name Jesus, because he will save his people from their sins."

Mathew 1:18-21

What a special selection of a humble woman to give birth to our Savior and redeemer! Indeed she is "blessed among women." One commentator states it right, *"No woman in the entire history of the world has been so honored and revered"*[12]

The virgin birth is one of the powerful demonstrations that God is supreme in all matters of life and death. God chooses and does what God wants to do. Biological human knowledge of life cannot contain, define or limit God when He moves into action. The story of Mary, the mother of Jesus is inspirational and challenging for us today. Her devotion and commitment to her son from birth, at the foot of the cross and the last mention when Jesus ascends to heaven is a powerful testimony and evidence of where God places women and their value in God's presence. The church today will be out of step with the truth if she attempts to remove women from their God given positions. Thank God for Mary, mother of Jesus Christ.

Peter's Mother-in-Law

When Jesus entered Peter's house, he saw his mother in law lying in bed with a fever; he touched her hand, and fever left her, and she got up and began to serve him, NRSV
Matthew 8:14-15

Jesus stopped from continuing on with his mission, and entered in the house of Peter to meet the needs of one woman who needed physical healing. As far as Jesus Christ is concerned, one woman's need is important enough to warrant the attention and ministry of the Son of God. That is what Jesus would have the church do today. Stop all your noise and high drama at worship; go outside your walls and seek to bring healing to one suffering, innocent victim of domestic violence and cultural abuse.

Jairus's Daughter and a Hemorrhaging Woman

When Jesus had crossed again in the boat to the other side, a great crowd gathered around him; and he was by the sea. Then one of the leaders of the synagogue named Jairus, came and, when he saw him, fell at his feet and begged him repeatedly, "My little daughter is at the point of death. Come and lay your hands on her, so that she may be made well, and live." So he went with him. And a large crowd followed him and pressed in on him. Now there was a woman who had been suffering from hemorrhages for twelve years. She had endured much under

*many physicians, and had spent all that she had; and was
no better, but rather grew worse. She had heard about
Jesus, and came up behind him in the crowd and touched
his cloak, for she said "If I but touch his clothes, I will be
made well." Immediately her hemorrhage stopped; and
she felt it in her body that she was healed of her disease.
Immediately aware that power had gone forth from him,
Jesus turned about in the crowd and said, "Who touched
my clothes? ...Daughter, your faith has made you well;
go in peace, and be healed of your disease."*

Mark 5:21-30, 34

Once more Jesus demonstrated what the new era was all about:
freedom, healing and wholeness for everyone, female and male
included. Jairus's daughter and the unnamed woman experienced
the master's healing touch. According to Hebrew tradition, Jesus
was not supposed to touch or be touched by this woman because she
was *unclean.* However, Jesus stops and publicly calls to her,
*"Daughter, your faith has made you well; go in peace, and be
healed of your disease."* Jesus demonstrated that the wrongs of the
past were being righted and no barriers are able to hold the daughter
of Israel in need of God's touch. Affirmation and healing is the
mission and message of the church today to women who have been
victimized by old and harmful cultural and tribal practices.

Jesus Visits a Widow in Nain

*Soon afterwards he went to a town called Nain, and his
disciples and a large crowd went with him. As he
approached the gate of the town, a man who had died was
being carried out. He was his mother's only son, and she
was a widow; and with her was a crowd from the town.
When the Lord saw her, he had compassion for her and
said to her, "Do not weep." Then he came forward and
touched the bier, and the bearers stood still. And he said,
"Young man, I say to you, rise!" The dead man sat up and
began to speak, and Jesus gave him his mother. Fear*

seized all of them; and they glorified God, saying "A great prophet has risen among us!" and "God has looked favorably on his people!" NRSV

Luke 7:11-16

Compassion, care, hope and the ability to restore the widow's son to life was the driving force in Jesus Christ. He exemplifies what the faith community should be about today, meeting the real needs of the oppressed among us.

The Crippled Woman

Now he was teaching in one of the synagogues on the Sabbath. And just then there appeared a woman with a spirit that had crippled her for eighteen years. She was bent over and was quite unable to stand up straight. When Jesus saw her, he called her over and said, "Woman you are set free from your ailment." When he laid his hands on her immediately she stood up straight and began praising God. But the leader of the synagogue, indignant because Jesus had cured on the Sabbath, kept saying to the crowd, "There are six days on which work ought to be done; come on those days and be cured, and not on the Sabbath day." But the Lord answered him and said, "You hypocrites! Does not each of you on the Sabbath untie his ox or his donkey from the manger, and lead it away to give it water? And ought not this woman, a daughter of Abraham whom Satan has bound for eighteen long years, be set free from this bondage on the Sabbath day?" When he said this, all his opponents were put to shame; and the entire crowd was rejoicing at all the wonderful things he was doing. NRSV

Luke 13:10-17

Jesus introduced a higher standard for diligent followers, putting the needs of people before legalistic requirements. Meeting the needs of our fellow sisters is the will of God in action. True righteousness is achieved by meeting needs, not by following a set of legalistic and inhuman requirements.

In this text, Jesus *violates* the then religious legal requirements to meet the needs of one woman. According to Jesus, this woman was bound by Satan for eighteen years while the legalistic religious systems did nothing for her. Jesus sets her free from bondage to demonstrate his mission and God's intent for the oppressed, spiritual and physical freedom.

The Giving Widow Luke 21:1-4

She is not named. Luke tells the reader that she was "*a poor widow*". Jesus elevated her because of her spiritual wealth demonstrated in her genuine giving of all her material possessions. The rich folks were challenged to emulate her as the spiritual standard and a living demonstration on the right attitude in giving. Her act of faith was used as a demonstration of how God expects us to give, selflessly and without a stingy heart.

The Woman and the Lost Coin Luke 15:8-10

Jesus uses a parable in which a woman is a model of what reconciliation with God is all about. Her diligence in looking for the coin, and celebration after it's found, illustrates what happens in the Kingdom of God when one lost individual is reconciled back to God.

The Persistent Widow Luke 18:1-8

Her enduring faith and steadiness stands against the judge who did not care about God or man. She is an illustration of what not losing heart in our spiritual struggles is all about. It's not the professional theologians or religious folks who "gets it." It's the "unschooled" pillars of faith, and beacons of hope who do, and Jesus Christ demonstrates this fact in the lives of these women.

The Widow of Zarephath Luke 4:24-26

Jesus reminds his audience about the Gentile woman in the town of Zarephath who in a time of need was a recipient of God's mercies. She was in a receptive mode and accepted the divine privilege of hosting the prophet Elijah. She was a Gentile woman, but this was irrelevant to Christ. Her faith and trust in God was outstanding and God had a special ministry for her.

The Samaritan Woman John 4:7-39

Jesus broke all the religious and cultural barriers and did what was culturally and politically incorrect. He decided to speak to a Samaritan woman in public, something the Jews were prohibited from doing. She in turn accepted him as a prophet and spread the word across her entire neighborhood.

Mary Magdalene Luke 8:1-3

Noted as one who had been cured by Jesus, she became a faithful follower of Jesus Christ and was present at his crucifixion. She is mentioned with other women of faith. Joanna and Susanna who were key participants in the ministry of Jesus Christ. God demonstrated to all persons of faith that gender differences were irrelevant in all matters of faith and practice.

Being masculine is not a special preference by God, but rather from a spiritual perspective calls for humility and use of one's gender uniqueness to serve God and humankind. Walls of division and manipulation along gender lines must come down to practically live out the proclamation of inclusion for all God's people. *There is neither male nor female for you are all one in Jesus Christ* (Galatians 3:28).

Other fascinating stories of women in the New Testament include, Elizabeth, mother of John the Baptist and Mary's cousin (Luke 1:5-13, 36-41,57), Anna, the daughter of Phanuel, the elderly prophetess who lived in the temple praying and worshiping the Lord. Luke powerfully describes her selfless devotion,

> *"There was also a prophetess, Anna, the daughter of Phanuel, of the tribe of Asher. She was very old; she had lived with her husband seven years after her marriage, and then was a widow until she was eighty-four. She never left the temple but worshiped night and day, fasting and praying."*

Luke 2:36-37

Eunice and Lois (2 Timothy 1:5) were two great women of faith who are credited for raising Timothy in a godly way. Eunice was the mother of Timothy and his grandmother was Lois. Three generations are represented in this short passage of Scripture, clearly showing that inter-generational parental influence is necessary to shape behavior. Similarly, in FGM, it will take godly women and men who will raise their children in godly ways eliminating all tribal and cultural harmful practices across generations. The same reflections on godly parenting can be applied to Salome (Mathew 20:20; 27:56; Mark 16:1-8) mother of James and John. She was a follower of Jesus up to the crucifixion and was at the tomb on that glorious resurrection morning. Lydia (Acts 16:14,40) was the first European Christian convert.

Lydia was also a successful businesswoman who responded to the preaching of Paul and herself and her entire household were baptized. She opened her home for the local church to assemble for worship, the first Christian center in Europe.

Dorcas also called Tabitha (Acts 9:36,39) provided sacrificially to the needs of the poor in the town of Joppa. Her death meant the end of all the much needed help for the poor, and some of those who had received garments from her sent for Paul to come and pray for her. Paul prayed for her and she rose from the dead. She was a symbol of generosity and good works out of her love for God and humanity.

The role and place of women is clearly articulated and demonstrated in the New Testament. The challenge is upon the community of faith to integrate women in the ministry of the Church and leadership positions in the community. Doing so will sensitize her members to be attentive to the voices of all the survivors and victims of female genital mutilation as they share their stories of pain, healing and hope.

In conclusion, let us move from talk to action; *"The freedom women found in the gospel was not mere wishful thinking...the foundation stone of Jesus' attitude toward women was his vision of them as persons to whom and for whom he had come."*[13] This understanding of a full liberating message of Jesus Christ to women will only be effective and have everlasting impact today if you and I internalize, digest and commit to practical daily living to the teachings of our master and savior Jesus Christ.

Chapter 6

RESEARCH, EDUCATION AND CONCLUSION

I n 1992 and 1996 the *Maendeleo Ya Wanawake* organization(a grassroots women's organization) in Kenya completed two significant studies: *"A Report on Harmful Traditional Practices that Affect the Health of the Women and their Children in Kenya"* and *"Qualitative Research Report On Female Circumcision In Four Districts In Kenya"*[1].

These studies offer important information and demonstrate the reluctance and discomfort in dealing with the subject. Overcoming the reluctance and calling the stakeholders into action will be a step in the right direction. The findings did have influence in encouraging the government's policy, but its the implementation of these policies that need work.

1992/1996 Research Findings

The two studies mentioned above represent some of the recent work of it's kind in Kenya that exhaustively *"documented the quantity, nature and locality of these traditions and practices."* The study listed some of the harmful traditional practices. Four different ethnic groups living in different parts of Kenya that practice female genital mutilation were selected for study. Meru, Samburu, Narok and Kisii districts participated in the study. The four districts occupy approximately the size of a congressional district in the United States. Sampled area participants were women 14 years of age and above. The Kenya central bureau of statistics assisted in the study design that targeted 1,200 women. The primary areas covered by the questionnaire included: child marriage, female genital mutilation, people's attitudes toward mutilated and non-mutilated females, and traditional taboos associated with nutrition. Illiteracy level among the respondents was between 61 and 91.4 per cent. Participating religious affiliations included Protestants, Catholics, Muslims, independent churches and traditional religions.

The relationship between religion and the practice of female genital mutilation by the sampled tribes in this study suggests that religious faith does not have any influence on the decision to mutilate or not to. The summary of this research study shows that 93 percent of Roman Catholics and 84 percent of Protestants residing in the four districts had undergone female genital mutilation. This clearly shows that religion is a significant factor to consider while looking at potential methods of educational outreach. The older the females, the higher the numbers were of those who had been mutilated. For example, 100 percent of all females over the age of 50 had been mutilated. The research further states that there were mixed feelings among women as to whether FGM should be eliminated or not. 65 percent favored its continuation and 35 percent were opposed. Such sentiments among women must be urgently addressed through education and aggressive outreach events at the grassroots level. There should never be room for compromise if this abusive practice will be discontinued. [2]

It is disturbing to note that this report suggests carrying out a *"less severe"* type of female genital mutilation. A mutilation is simply a mutilation. It an extreme form of violence against girls and women that must be eradicated. According to the statistics provided, there is no difference between religious and non-religious participants in these interviews. They all support and practice FGM. The potential for the religious communities to effectively teach their members has never been better than now, with the national media carrying news and letters from readers about the subject. Public openness to dialogue on this subject should not be taken lightly but fully exploited by the religious communities in spearheading this battle. In the same research they questioned why these women chose to be mutilated (for those who were old enough to choose), over 84 percent responded by stating that, it was *"good tradition"* and a *"sign of maturity from childhood to adulthood."*

Another important aspect revealed by this data includes the reasons FGM should be eradicated. The two major reasons identified as to why eradication is necessary were *"against human rights and woman's dignity"* and *"it is prohibited by religion.* Once more the human rights aspects of FGM seem to be clearly understood, which is closely followed by religion. While the Bible does not literally mention female genital mutilation, it identifies violence as a sin and biblical teachings are against unjust treatment of the helpless and especially young, defenseless children. Religious communities have the advantage of access to the people; hence pastoral care education from a faith perspective grounded in human rights will be an effective combination in the education and awareness efforts.

Respondents who favored the elimination of this evil described the excruciating pain during the operation. They believed that the amount of pain caused is not worthy of the cultural claims of its value. Respondents identified education as the number one weapon to fight against FGM, especially targeting fathers and challenging them to protect their daughters against this evil. Legislative work whereby laws would be enacted to make it a crime to mutilate girls [3] was second in this category.

Another qualitative research project by the *Maendeleo Ya Wanawake Organization*, jointly sponsored by the Program for Appropriate Technology in Health (PATH), was completed in 1996. The intent was to conduct a qualitative research on female circumcision in four Kenyan districts.[4] The report submitted six recommendations:

(i). *Additional research should be conducted with a larger sample in areas where female circumcision is still prevalent to examine in greater detail gender issues related to circumcision. Results of the research would be used to convince government officials of the need to eradicate female circumcision and to solicit funding from donors to implement interventions.*

(ii). *Concerned groups should initiate social mobilization campaigns in areas where research has already been conducted to create awareness of the health consequences of female circumcision.*

(iii). *Information, education, and communication materials should be adapted from existing materials or developed to support and strengthen social mobilization campaigns.*

(iv). *Alternative activities should be identified and introduced to replace female circumcision, but retain the cultural significance of the event.*

(v). *Maendeleo Ya Wanawake Organization (MWYO) should disseminate existing data in areas where research was conducted to seek support for and incorporate eradication of female circumcision as a gender and female reproductive health issue.*

(vi). *Women's organizations in Kenya should work in collaboration to intensify efforts to create awareness in other women of traditional practices that adversely affect their health and active participation in social, education, political, and economic issues in the community.*

The 1996 research findings were similar to 1992 in the sense that they both highlighted the central role of tribal loyalty to this ritual and the impact of education that is enabling potential victims to start questioning the value of these rituals. Eradication remains the final goal, and these two research outcomes are great strides in the right direction in ending FGM practice [5].

The above conclusion provides clear and concise suggestions toward the eradication of FGM. The opportunities for the faith community in Kenya are enormous through Sunday school curriculums, youth ministry programs, catechism classes, courtship mentoring, premarital and marital counseling, youth conventions, and social clubs. Recent FGM research in Sierra Leone sheds more light for the rest of Africa. The suggested eradication model follows ten steps: Rehabilitation, intentional programming, medical care of victims, legal measures against perpetrators, alternate rites of passage, bioethical lessons on genital mutilations, and comprehensive follow up programs for potential victims.[6]

The above plan of action is holistic and very adaptable in other African communities. Training small groups of clergy, medical personnel and youth leaders as a mobile interdisciplinary unit team have the potential of producing short and long-term results. Home grown indigenous teams will have moral authority and credibility with their audiences. Resistance can be expected, but there are great benefits in building alliances and networks in the local village churches, schools and health care centers at the heart of where these mutilations take place. Empowered FGM survivors who are not ashamed to tell their stories of shame and pain will have the opportunity to share life-changing stories with those who have not been mutilated. Supporting these testimonies with medical/psychological and health care evidence based on research findings in this field will be a powerful tool that will assist in dismantling the foundations of erroneous tribal and cultural beliefs.

A presentation from the religious perspective by the clergy detailing the unconditional repentance and seeking forgiveness for the silence in midst of torture of the innocents will offer immediate and accessible pastoral care support for victims seeking to start their long journey to wellness.

There is a renewed level of openness in Kenya today and the government must be commended for her efforts in raising public awareness through the former state controlled television. For example on 5 January 2002 at 7.30pm, the Kenya Broadcasting Corporation (KBC) broadcasted one of its popular programs, *Vioja Mahakamani,* a television drama program showing a court scene with the prosecutor, the criminal and the judge in place. That night, the criminal was an elderly woman who had forcibly mutilated her daughter. She argued that although her daughter was only in standard eight (eighth grade), she was going to be cut and immediately get married in an arranged marriage setting. She adamantly refused to listen to the learned female judge and ended up receiving a jail sentence for six months. As she left the docket, she was verbally protesting, stating that she would continue with the practice after doing time in jail. Such programs will gradually eliminate the taboo, shame of public debate on the subject and the secrecy surrounding female genital mutilation. The results will be public openness and willingness to defend the innocent and helpless victims.

Another encouraging step by the government was the signing of the Children's Bill, whereby it will be a criminal offense for anybody to mutilate a girl aged sixteen and below. According to media reports, the Children's Bill provides one year in jail and/or a fine of up to 50,000.00 Kenya Shillings (approximately $650.00 US dollars). While this is a good news story, putting this law into practice will be a significant challenge just as it is with other laws in Kenya where a criminal can buy his way out of jail due to the chronic bribery in the judicial system.

A new government was elected into office in December 2003 and has vowed to wipe out corruption. Kenya is pregnant with very high hopes and some of those elected into office include a strong group of women who have been advocates and champions against FGM. Now that they are in the government, legislation against cruel practices like FGM stand a chance of coming to the floor of the parliament and passing into law. Time will tell.

CONCLUSION

"Without forgiveness there is no future."
Archbishop Desmond Tutu (South Africa)

Eradication Goals

The author's intent was to accomplish five goals:

    (i).   Provide a historical survey background of FGM in selected African countries, with a special focus on Kenya.

    (ii). Describe the role of gender inequality, domestic violence, and abuse against innocent girls and women and their roots and influence on FGM.

    (iii). Raise the awareness of psychological, medical and sexual impact on the victims of female genital mutilation.

    (iv). Demonstrate biblical, theological, cultural and pastoral care implications to sensitize the communities of faith to accept their role in breaking the culture of silence and compromise.

(v). Offer a suggested pastoral care education response to FGM and other educational resources available to assist in the elimination efforts.

Eradication of FGM will take long-term, consistent, interdisciplinary efforts by all the communities of faith. The medical community and women-led nongovernmental organizations in Africa can significantly assist in the struggle through consistent funding and sponsoring of local interdisciplinary education groups doing outreach work. Understanding the medical complications of FGM and teaching every girl child in seminars, houses of worship and quarterly resident schools will be a significant step in this process.

The author's suggested plan of eradication focuses on building ministry teams in every location in Kenya. The suggested name would be, Religious & Health Care Alliance (RHCA). The Alliance would be able to recruit members from all walks of life, especially clergy, medical doctors and nongovernmental organizations, especially *Maendeleo ya Wanawake* at the grassroots levels. Each team would liaison with local health officials, religious leaders and government officials, especially assistant chiefs and chiefs to conduct seminars in local churches and health centers.

In May 2002 the first female assistant chief was appointed among the Maasai community of Kenya, and this will help in the fight against female genital mutilation and early arranged marriages for innocent, unsuspecting girls among the Maasai people. Many victims have been married off to polygamists, older men in their fifties and above.

For the first time, over ten women were elected into office and hold high positions in the new Kenyan government. One of the elected officials has been an ardent supporter against FGM. Hope is very high that these strong women of faith will lead the charge against all practices that discriminate against women. In Appendix I and II there are two bills passed by both the United Kingdom House of Parliament and the United States Congress banning female genital mutilation.

Kenya will hopefully lead the way in Africa by publishing into law prohibitions against female genital mutilation and ruthlessly enforce this law. In places where women are in leadership, a posi-tive response may result faster than elsewhere. The RHCA team can systematically visit from one village to another within the Districts, armed with audiovisual equipment to actually show what happens during female genital mutilation. A drama group can literally act the mutilation ceremony out with an instructor, explaining the impact of the mutilation step by step. Making short video presentations with actual mutilation scenarios using local languages and later demon-strating the aftermath of FGM will leave an everlasting memory in the lives of the participants, producing change. Being able to demonstrate and show the damage done to the female genitalia is a critical step in the education process.

Shame and secrecy around the subject must be eliminated through graphic demonstrations of what happens during a mutila-tion event. Target population can be active church members first, followed by public and private schools, colleges and university communities.

In every sub location in Kenya, there are between three and five religious communities, a health center, primary school, and some have secondary school facilities. These offer an available infrastructure to operate within. Effective intervention at the village level will build a strong foundation all the way up to the provincial and national level. Starting from the bottom up can be the most effective option in Kenya, allowing the transformation process to start from the victim's environment.

The primary intervention and eradication lessons will be built from pastoral and health care perspectives. Active participation by local medical doctors, pastors, lawyers and women professionals from all walks of life will offer the variety and expertise this subject demands. The curriculum may include the following topics:

(i). Understanding trauma and healing in female genital mutilation.
(ii). Female anatomy and sexual functioning, fulfillment and FGM.
(iii). Human beings as God's design and creation.

(iv). Definitions of cultural practices and human rights abuse.

(v). Outline the new Children's Bill and it's legal consequences.

(vi). Non-violent alternatives to abusive and violent rites of passage.

(vii). Spiritual implications of spouse and child abuse.

(viii). Pastoral care and counseling of FGM victims.

(ix). Practical steps to empowerment of women living in cultural and tribal bondage and how to break free.

(x). Public health policy and non-violent actions at the village level.

A model project currently underway in a local church in the Rift Valley province of Kenya is using drama and art to teach local villagers the dangers of FGM. Lessons are taught by the local church elders following a step by step analysis of all the dangers faced by FGM victims. The parents are challenged to dialogue on the advantages and disadvantages of female genital mutilation in an open forum inside the church building. Finally, they are asked to come up with an alternative ritual to mark the rite of passage from childhood that is not violent like FGM. This is a great effort and deserves to be supported and adopted by other communities.

Another local educational effort is within the Seventh Adventist Church in western Kenya; church leaders are discouraging parents from conducting FGM.[7]. The first step was at the grassroots whereby 250 parents of potential female candidates for mutilation were recently brought together in a joint seminar with medical personnel. The presentation covered the risks of HIV/AIDS and Hepatitis B during circumcision. Currently the Seventh Day Adventist (SDA) Church is working on a curriculum to teach alternative rites of passage.

In Meru, eastern Kenya, an alternative rite of passage to FGM ritual was introduced in 1996. The rite is locally known as *"Ntanira na Mugambo,"* or *"circumcision through words."* There are three key elements involved: society celebration, affirmation and counseling. The entire event takes one week. Emphasis is on the cultural significance of the transition from childhood to young adulthood and accompanying responsibilities. Other subjects of instruction include self-esteem, communication, personal hygiene, and reproductive health factors.[8]

Female anatomy and sexual matters are considered very personal, private and in some communities taboo to discuss in public. The intervention team members must be sensitive when dealing with the different age groups whose understanding, education and openness to discuss FGM may be limited. Patience, understanding, wisdom and tact will come in handy. Older age groups are most likely to produce aggressive resistance and would probably refuse to discuss the subject. The resistance can be shocking especially when coming from a potential victim as reported recently in a local Kenyan newspaper. A school girl in West Pokot, threatened to commit suicide if her parents refused her to be mutilated. This is one example of how deep tribal roots and beliefs in FGM run among different communities. Having a readily available residential environment where such girls can go for several months of training and counseling would turn the tide on this barbaric practice.

Long-term education and time is of the essence if female genital mutilation will be demolished and eliminated in Africa. It is widely believed that education is finally paying off among the Gikuyu community of central Kenya where statistics suggest that female genital mutilation is as low as 15 percent in a community that mutilated their girls ten years ago at about 75 percent. It will take an equivalent of a cultural conversion experience to fully digest the dangers of female genital mutilation and the need to stop it. Patience is required in this process, but this does not mean silence. In the same region of Kenya, West Pokot, 153 girls aged between 10 and 18 underwent an alternative rite of passage saving them from the brutality. The rite of passage ceremony was held in Cheparreria Girls High School. The method followed in this intervention above, matches closely with the ten step course of action suggested by the author above. Health personnel and teachers combined their efforts in educating the girls on reproductive health issues and the dangers of genital mutilation. The community at large is slowly accepting the fact that FGM is harmful to society. More needs to be done in outreach intervention.

Other programs of similar nature are currently underway in Narok, Kajiado, Meru and Trans Mara districts. There will be success stories and some setbacks where some of these graduates might be sneaked out at night and mutilated against their wishes by the money-hungry parents who want to marry off their daughters in a hurry to make easy money. This battle must continue and will be won some day, and I pray not too far in the future.

Another good news story appeared in the *Daily Nation* newspaper, reporting that a father in Eldoret town, was permanently stopped by the court from forcing his two daughters from facing the knife. 9. The girls sought assistance from a local center for human rights and democracy in Eldoret town. This is very encouraging to note that education is paying dividends in empowering individuals to stand up for themselves and seek help without shame or fear. According to this report, this was a major victory for young people who will definitely be empowered and energized to stand for their rights. The older tribal members were reportedly dissatisfied with the courts' ruling barring the father permanently from forcing his two girls to be mutilated. May these stories of victory continue to be told and retold in a contagious way, spreading the good news and empowering young people into taking a stand.

International involvement is required in this eradication process through empowering of local groups on the ground. The United Nations International Children's Fund (UNICEF) should feel compelled to lead the way in education and especially in funding resources at the village level. For example, the German nongovernmental organization (German Technical Cooperation) GTZ is currently leading efforts in funding education projects in Kenya. Their project is entitled, *Promotion of Initiatives to Overcome Female Genital Mutilation*. Their focus is teaching principles and values of womanhood, especially among the Maasai community.

Effective education will only get under way when all the rural and urban Islamic, Catholic, Protestants and traditional religious leaders team up with other community organizations in this war. Opening worship centers for education and eradication efforts will pay great dividends. Legislative efforts are the least effective in winning the war, but the outreach teams should not shy away from showing the legal consequences of those who choose to continue with the mutilations.

Forgiveness

The smart weapon of our warfare will be holistic education from a pastoral care perspective using a practical and systematic plan of action at the village level. Forgiveness will be the last step necessary in the pastoral care process. However, the victims should be empowered enough to define what forgiveness means for them. The following understanding of forgiveness suggests a new way of understanding forgiveness;

> ... *forgiveness in today's culture is perceived to have meanings ranging from the forgetting of what has happened to the making of everything "OK" again, that is, as though it never happened (Appendix A). These definitions mean the offense "becomes a non offense" (Fortune, 1983, p.208). For the person who has experienced abuse, these explanations are not enough, neither are they valid, as no explanation will turn their experience into a nonoffense... Forgiveness, as an experience of grace, permits humanity, its imperfections, frailties, and shortcomings, and yet continues to call humanity to account for the injustice, disrespect, and disregard it shows one another. Forgiveness, as an experience of grace, opens up possibilities by not denying anyone the opportunity to experience it. When understood in this way, forgiveness moves from being a one way action or an issue of power over and above another, to being a parallel journey with the Divine."*[10]

Justice, wholeness of life, experiencing grace, healing and restoration are the long-term goals in the struggle. The ability to fully comprehend the nature and extent of FGM as an offense and a crime against women is necessary; it is a crime against women, and the legal system must write it in their books. The author believes forgiveness in reference to FGM is a process, and a journey that cannot be rushed. It should be the last and vital step from a pastoral care perspective in the eradication process. The victims will be able to forgive those who have done them this immense wrong. However, they will never forget it. The physical mark will stay permanently on the body and in her soul. Archbishop Desmond Tutu (retired) of South Africa is right in saying:

"Forgiveness is not just some nebulous, vague idea that one can easily dismiss. Forgiveness is taking seriously the awfulness of what has happened when you are treated unfairly...without forgiveness resentment builds in us, a resentment that turns into hostility and anger... Forgiveness is not cheap. It is facing the ghastliness of what has happened and giving the other person the opportunity of coming out of that ghastly situation. We must forgive, but almost always we should not forget that there were atrocities, because if we do, we are then likely to repeat these atrocities. Those who forgive and those who accept forgiveness must not forget in their reconciling, without forgiveness there is no future."[11]

Victims of female genital mutilation will forever bear the physical mark inflicted on them by their perpetrators. The wound will eventually heal, and the psychological pain will gradually ease. However, our sisters will never forget the atrocities and crimes committed against them. May their memories energize, empower and inspire the vision of elimination of female genital mutilation and all other forms of domestic violence against the girl child and the women of Africa. Amen!

PROHIBITION OF FEMALE GENITAL MUTILATION IN THE UNITED KINGDOM

HER MAJESTY QUEEN ELIZABETH II PROHIBITION OF FEMALE CIRCUMCISION ACT OF 1985 IN THE UNITED KINGDOM[1]

PROHIBITION OF FEMALE CIRCUMCISION ACT 1985
CHAPTER 33
An act to prohibit female circumcision. [16th July 1985]

BE IT ENACTED by the Queen's most Excellent Majesty, by and with the advice and consent of the Lord's Spiritual and Temporal. And Commons, in their present Parliament assembled, and by authority of the same, as follows:-

Subject to section 2 below, it shall be an offence for any person to excise, infibulate or otherwise mutilate the whole or any part of the labia majora or clitoris of another person; or to aid, abet, counsel or procure the performance by another person of any of those acts on that other person's own body.

A person guilty of an offence under this section shall be liable —on conviction of indictment to a fine or to imprisonment for a term not exceeding five years or to both; or on summary conviction, to a fine not exceeding the statutory maximum (as defined in section 74 of the Criminal Justice act 1982) or to imprisonment for a term not exceeding six months, or to both.

This act may be cited as the Prohibition of Female Circumcision Act 1985.

PROHIBITION OF FEMALE GENITAL MUTILATION IN THE UNITED STATES

UNITED STATES 103RD CONGRESS BILL NUMBER (FGM), H.R.3075 TO PROHIBIT FEMALE GENITAL MUTILATION IN THE UNITED STATES OF AMERICA AS INTRODUCED IN THE HOUSE—BILL H.R. 3075 SEPTEMBER 14, 1993

TITLE: To promote greater equity in the delivery of health care services to American women through expanded research on women's health Issues and through improved access to health care services, including preventive health services.

SUBTITLE M—FEDERAL PROHIBITION OF FEMALE GENITAL MUTILATION OF 1993

SEC. 261. SHORT TITLE.

This subtitle may be cited as the 'Federal Prohibition of Female Genital Mutilation Act of 1993'.

SEC. 262. TITLE 18 AMENDMENT

(a) In General—Chapter 7 of title 18, United States Code, is amended by adding at the end the following new section: 'Sec.116. Female Genital Mutilation'

(a) Except as provided in subsection (b), whoever knowingly circumcises, excises, or infibulates the whole or any part of the labia majora or labia minora or clitoris of another person who has not attained the age of 18 years shall be fined under this title or imprisoned not more than 5 years, or both.

   (b) A surgical operation is not a violation of this section if the operation is -

   (1) necessary to the health of the person on whom it is performed, and is performed by a person licensed in the place of its performance as a medical practitioner; or

   (2) performed on a person in labor or who has just given birth and is performed for medical purposes connected with that labor or birth by a person licensed in the place it is performed as a medical practitioner, midwife, or person in training to become such a practitioner or midwife.

   (c) In applying subsection (b) (1), no account shall be taken of the effect on the person on whom the operation is to be performed of any belief on the part of that or any other person that the operation is required as a matter of custom or ritual.

   (d) Whoever knowingly denies to any person medical care or services or otherwise discriminates against any person in the provision of medical care or services, because -

   (1) that person has undergone female circumcision, excision, or infibulation; or that person has requested that female circumcision, excision, or infibulation be performed on any person; shall be fined under this title or imprisoned not more than one year, or both.

(b) Clerical Amendment. The table of sections at the beginning of chapter 7 of title 18, United States Code, is amended by adding at the end the following new item:
'116. Female Genital Mutilation'.

SEC. 263. EDUCATION AND OUTREACH.

The Secretary of Health and Human Services shall carry out appropriate education, preventive, and outreach activities in communities that traditionally practice female circumcision, excision, or infibulation, to inform people in those communities about the health risks and emotional trauma inflicted by those practices, and to inform them and the medical community about the provisions of section 262.

SEC. 264. EFFECTIVE DATES

Section 263 shall take effect immediately, and the Secretary of Health and Human Services shall commence carrying it out not later than 90 days after the date of the enactment of the Act. Section 262 shall take effect 180 days after the date of the enactment of this Act.

Appendix III

SUGGESTED QUESTIONS FOR FGM SURVIVORS FOR FURTHER RESEARCH

1. What is the name of your (ethnic) group?
2. Who is circumcised in your ethnic group?
3. Why do you circumcise them?
4. In what ways are boys' and girls' circumcisions different?
5. At what age are girls circumcised ? Why?
6. How is it done, in a group or just individually?
7. How is the operation done? What do you think about it? How does that make you feel?
8. Do you like it? Why? What would happen to uncircumcised girls?
9. What kind of a person would she grow up to be? Is it bad?
10. What are the tools used?
11. Who decides that the girls should get circumcised?
12. Are there prior preparations before the girl is circumcised?
13. What are they?
14. Who prepares?
15. Who performs the operation? How much do they charge?
16. Where is it done?
17. Are the operation tools sterilized? Used many times?
18. What does the operation involve?
19. What part(s) is removed?
20. Do they apply any medication? If yes, which one?

Appendix IV

QUESTIONS FOR FGM SUPPORTERS (PARENTS, GRAND PARENTS AND OTHER FAMILY MEMBERS) ACTIVELY INVOLVED IN FGM

1. Is female circumcision practiced in your community?
2. How widespread is the practice (i.e. does everyone do it)? Why? Does it have a different meaning for girls as opposed to boys?
3. At what age do you circumcise your girls and why?
4. At what age do you circumcise your boys and why?
5. Is it done communally or individually?
6. What season/time of the year is circumcision done and why?
7. Where is circumcision performed?
8. Who performs circumcision and what equipment is used?
9. What preparations do you make for your daughters prior to the circumcision?
10. How is the female circumcision done? Who is the person who holds the girls? What does that mean to her and to her family?
11. Who takes care of the initiates and where do they stay?
12. How long do they stay there and what do they do during this time?
13. If they received FLE (Family Life Education) how is it communicated to them and by whom?
14. Why do they cut those parts of the female organs?
15. Why does your community circumcise girls?
16. Are there communities which do not circumcise girls? What happens to the uncircumcised girls?

17. Is it the girl who discloses to her parents when she wishes circumcision or is it the parents who decide?
18. Who pays the circumciser? How much and why?
19. As a grandmother, father, mother, what is your role and why?
20. Do you ever encounter resistance to female circumcision from your girls?
21. How is this (resistance) dealt with and by whom?
21. What are your feelings towards female circumcision? Are you for it? Yes, no, why?
22. Has anyone ever heard anything bad about circumcising girls? What have you heard? How does that make you feel?
23. If someone said that circumcision causes unnecessary pain to girls, how would you feel? What would you say to them?
24. How do your daughters benefit from female circumcision?
25. Why is female circumcision practiced in the manner you described previously?
26. What is the significance of the preparation before female circumcision?
27. Is there any difference in the child's attitude after her circumcision? Why?
28. How is a girl expected to behave after circumcision? Why?
29. What is the general feeling towards uncircumcised girls in the community?
30. Why are they not circumcised?

ENDNOTES

[1]Charles L. Whitefield, *Memory And Abuse: Remembering And Healing The Effects of Trauma,* Health Communications Publishers, Deerfield Beach, Florida, 1995.

[2]Raqiya Haji Dualeh Abdalla, *Sisters, Sisters In Affliction. Circumcision and Infibulation of Women in Africa,* Lawrence Hill and Company, Connecticut, 1982, 7.

[3]Nahid Toubia, '*Female Genital Mutilation as a Public Health Issue,*' The New England Journal of Medicine 11, (Vol 331 Fall 1994), 712.

[4]A Joint WHO/UNICEF/UNFPA Statement, *Female Genital Mutilation* (Geneva: World Health Organization, 1997), 3.

[5]Efua Dorkenoo, and Scilla Elworthy, *Female Genital Mutilation: Proposals for Change,* Minority Rights International Report. P.7.

[6]The Female Genital Mutilation Home Page, 1997, (accessed 11 November 1997), available from http://www.fgm.com; Internet.

[7]Ibid.

[8]Joceylyn Margaret Murray, *The Kikuyu Female Circumcision Controversy With Special Reference to The Church Missionary Society's "Sphere of Influence"* (Michigan: University Microfilms, 1974).

[9]Joseph Cathy, *"Compassionate Accountability: An Embodied Consideration of Female Genital Mutilation,"* Journal of Psychohistory 11 (Summer 1996) 2-17

[10]Masters and Johnson, *Masters and Johnson On Sex and Human Loving.* 1991. P.3

Chapter 1—Female Genital Mutilation and the Patriarchy

[1]Hilary Ng'weno, 'Sexism In Kenya', *The Weekly Review* (August 1991): 6

[2]Okot P' Bitek, *'Woman from Kikuyuland'*, The Daily Nation Online Newspaper; available at http://www.africaonline.co.ke. dailynation.html; Internet; accessed 10 November 97.

[3]G Baara, *One Thousand Kikuyu Proverbs*, (Nairobi: Kenya Literature Bureau, 1939), 6-122

[4]Wanjiku Mukabi Kabira, *Democratic Change In Africa*, 25-33.

Chapter 2—Stories of Terror and Pain

[1]Parents Magazine, *'Death in Circumcision'* February 1991, 16-18.

[2]*Independent on Sunday*, Egyptian Newspaper, 25 August 1996.

[3]Mohammed Badawi, M.D., MPH, Epediology of Female Sexual Castration in Cairo, Egypt, unpublished Research Paper (Accessed 10 December 1998), available from http://www.nocirc.org/symposia/first/badawi.html; internet.

[4]Ibid.

[5]*Origin of Circumcision*, (accessed 11 November 97), available from http://www.fgm homepage.

[6]Elworthy and Dorkenoo, *Female Genital Mutilation: Proposals for Change,* page 8.

[7]Reuters News Agency. 12 January 1997.

[8]Hawid Rushwan, 'Female Circumcision', University of Khartoum, Sudan. *World Health, The magazine of the World Health Organization.* Geneva, Switzerland, March 1990. P.24-25

[9]Celia W. Dugger, 'Woman Asylum, Endures Prison in America', *The New York Times*, (accessed 23 March 1998); available from http://www.nytimes.com; internet.

[10]Sylvia Moreno, 'Nigerian Woman Gets Asylum Hearing', *The Washington Post,* (accessed 7 October 1998); available from http://www.spokane.net; Internet.

[11]Stella Babalola and Christine Adebajo. Evaluation Report of Female Circumcision Eradication Project in Nigeria. (Unpublished Paper). Project Implemented by the National

Association of Nigerian Nurses and Midwives with technical assistance by Program for Appropriate Technology for Health (PATH). 1987-1990.p.26.

Chapter 3—Religion and Violence

[1]Memorandum Prepared by the Mission Council of the Church of Scotland, *'Kenya, Female Circumcision'*, 1931.

[2]Margaret Murray, *'The Kikuyu Female Circumcision Controversy'*, 1974. pp.163-165.

[3]Ibid, note 1 above.

[4]The Rev. W.P. Knapp is buried in Kenya outside one of the Church compound in Kambui, Central Kenya. The author of this book was a teacher in Kambui Girls High School and visited Rev. Knapp's gravesite in 1989.

[5]Ibid, note 1 above, p.60-61.

Chapter 4—Psychological, Medical and Sexual Consequences

[1]Judith Herman, *Trauma and Recovery. The Aftermath of Violence from Domestic Abuse to Political Terror.* New York. Basic Books, 1997, p.33.

[2]Charles R. Figley. *Helping Traumatized Families.* San Francisco, Jossey-Bass Publishers, 1989, p.39.

[3]Charles L. Whitefield. *Memory and Abuse: Remembering and Healing the Effects of Trauma.* Florida, Health Communications Inc, 1995, p.231.

[4]Diana Sullivan Everstine and Louis Everstine. *The Trauma Response: Treatment for Emotional Injury.* New York, W.W. Norton & Company, 1993, p.ix-3.

[5]American Psychiatric Association. Diagnostic and Statistical Manual of Mental Disorders (DSM-IV). Washington DC, American Psychiatric Association, 1994.

[6]Hamid Rushwan. Female Circumcision In Sudan: University of Khartoum, World Health. The Magazine of the World Health Organization. Geneva, Switzerland, 1990, p.24-25.

[7]Female Genital Mutilation. A Joint WHO/UNICEF/UNFPA Statement. Geneva, 1997. p.8.

[8]Efua Dorkenoo, *Cutting The Rose. Female Genital Mutilation. The Practice and Its Prevention.* London: Minority Rights Group Publishers, 1995, p.7.

[9]Kowser H. Omer-Hashi, 'Midwife Commentary: Female Genital Mutilation; Perspectives from a Somalian Midwife', *Birth Issues In Perinatal Care* 21, December 1994, p.224-225.

[10]Robert Karen, 'Shame', *The Atlantic Monthly*, 1 February 1992, p.50-60.

[11]Francis J. Broucek, Shame and the Self. London. Guilford Press, 1982, p.28.

[12]Dr. Badawi. "Female Castration In Egypt". Accessed 10 December 1998; available from http:www.fgm.com; internet.

[13]Joint WHO/UNICEF/UNFPA Statement, Geneva, 1997, p.7.

[14]Allison Shorten. 'Female Circumcision. Understanding Special Needs'. Holistic Nursing Practice 2, January 1995, p.66-73.

[15]Paul Bimal Kanti. Maternal Mortality In Africa, 1980-87, *Social Science Journal & Medicine An International Journal* 6, September 1993, p.745-752.

[16]Ibid, note 15 above.

[17]Female Circumcision: Obstetrics Issues, *'American Journal of Obstetrics & Gynaecology* 4', October 1993, p.1616-1618.

[18]Ibid, note 17 above.

[19]M.A. Dirie and G. Lindmark, "The Risk of Medical Complications After Female Circumcision', East African medical Journal 1, January 1992, p.479-483.

[20]Evelyn Shaw, 'Female Circumcision. What kind of Maternity Care do Circumcised Women Need? And can United States Caregivers Provide it?, American Journal of Nursing, June 1985, p.684-687.

[21]L.F. Lowenstein, 'Attitudes and Attitudes Differences to Female Genital Mutilation in the Sudan, Is there Change in the Horizon?, Social Science & Medicine 5A, February 1978, p.417-421.

[22]Ibid, note 12 above.

[23]Female Circumcision is Terrible, *The Daily Nation*, 20 December 1996, p.2.

[24]Lowenstein, 'An overview of some aspects of female sexuality', *Social Casework*, February 1978.

[25]bid, *Social Casework,* 1978.

Chapter 5—Pastoral Care In Female Genital Mutilation

[1]Pamela Cooper-White, *The Cry of Tamar: Violence Against Women and the Church's Response*, Minneapolis: Fortress Press, 1995.

[2]Ibid. Pamela Cooper-White.

[3]Maxine Glaz., Jeanne Stevenson Moessner. *Women in Travail and Transition, A New Pastoral Care,* Minneapolis, Fortress Press, 1991, p.136.

[4]Marshall M. Fortune, *Sexual Violence. The Unmentionable Sin. An Ethical Perspective,* Ohio: Pilgrim Press, 1983, xii-xiii.

[5]The term holistic education refers to an approach that will include basic theological and biological perspectives on female anatomy. Understanding the creative power and wisdom of God in all the body parts and their functions is critical. Medical practitioners must be involved in this process and together with clergy weave the type of a curriculum that will address the question why genital mutilation is unnecessary. The community of faith must listen carefully to their sacred Scriptures, songs, prayers, and clearly articulate and identify with the survivor's pain.

[6]Gilbert Bilezikian, *Beyond Sex Roles: What the Bible Says About a Woman's place In Church and Family*, Grand Rapids, Michigan: Baker Book House, 1996. P.23.

[7]The Bible, New Revised Standard Version, unless otherwise stated.

[8]Ibid, note 6 above.

[9]Judy Mbugua, *Our Time Has Come. African Christian Women Address The Issues of Today*, Grand Rapids, Michigan: Baker Book House, 1994, p. 68.

[10] Alice Ogden Bellis, *Helpmates Harlots Heroes: Women's Stories In the Hebrew Bible*, Louisville, Kentucky: John Knox/ Westminster Press, 1994, p.90.

[11] Ibid, note 10 above.

[12]Edith Deen. All The Women of The Bible. New York, New York: Harper and Row Publishers, 1955, p.156.

[13]Stanley J. Grenz., Denise M. Kjesbo. Women In the Church: A Biblical Theology of Women in Ministry, Downers Grove, Illinois, Intervarsity press, 1995, p.80-87

Chapter 6—Research and Education Efforts in Kenya

[1]*Maendeleo ya Wanawake* is a Swahili term meaning, "The development of women". This is a national level nongovernmental organization in Kenya with goals to improve the lives of women in both urban and rural areas.

[2]Maendeleo Ya Wanawake Report, A Report on Harmful Traditional Practices That Affects the Health of Women and their Children in Kenya, 1992, p.4-5.

[3]Ibid. Maendeleo Ya Wanawake Report.

[4]Program for Appropriate Technology in Health (PATH/Kenya). *Qualitative Research Report on Female Circumcision in Four Districts in Kenya*, Maendeleo Ya Wanawake, 7 August 1996.

[5]Ibid, note 2 above.

[6]Koso Olanyika Thomas, *The Circumcision of Women. A Strategy for Eradication,* Trowbridge-Wiltshire, United Kingdom, Dotesios Publishers Limited, 1992, p.71-73.

[7]*The Daily Nation*, 'Church Opposes Female Ritual', 4 October 1998.

[8]*Alternative Rite to Female Circumcision Spreading in Kenya*, Africa Online, available at http://www.africanews.org/specials/19971119-fgm.html. Accessed 9 September 1998.

[9]The Daily Nation, *'Man's Bid to Circumcise Daughter is Blocked'*. 14 December 2000.

[10]Robert D. Enright., Joana North. *Exploring Forgiveness*. Madison, Wisconsin, University of Wisconsin Press, 1998.

[11]Ibid, note 9 above.

Appendix I

[1]W.J.Sharp. *Acts of Parliament.* London, United Kingdom: Her Majesty's Publishers, 1985.

Appendix II

[1]United States Congress Unofficial Version of a Bill (Washington, DC, 1997, accessed 7 October 1998) ; available from http://www.eskimo.com/gburlin/female.html; Internet.

Appendix III

[1]Maendeleo Ya Wanawake Organization, *"A Report on Harmful Practices that affect the Health of Women and their Children in Kenya,"* Nairobi, Kenya: 1992°

Appendix IV

[1]Maendeleo Ya Wanawake Organization, *"A Report on Harmful Practices that affect the Health of Women and their Children in Kenya,"* Nairobi, Kenya: 1992

BIBLIOGRAPHY

Abdalla, Raqiya. *Sisters in Affliction. Circumcision and Infibulation of Women in Africa.* London: Zed Press, 1982.

Adagala Kavetsa and Kabira Wanjiku. *Kenyan Oral Narratives.* Nairobi: Heineman Educational Books, 1985.

Atkinson, David. *The Message Of Genesis 1-11.* Downers Grove, Illinois: Intervarsity Press, 1990.

Baker, C.A., G.J. Gilson., M.D. Vill, and L.B. Curet. "Female Circumcision: Obstetric Issues." *American Journal Of Obstetrics And Gynaecology*, (December 1993) : 1616-1618.

Baara, G. *1000 Gikuyu Proverbs.* Nairobi: Kenya Literature Bureau, 1939.

Bellis, O.A. *Helpmates Harlots Heroes. Women's Stories In The Hebrew Bible.* Louisville, Kentucky: John Knox Press, 1994.

Brock, Nakashima R. *Journeys By Heart.* New York: Crossroad Publications, 1988.

Broucek, Francis J. *Shame And The Self.* London: Guilford Press, 1991.

Bilezikian, G. *Beyond Sex Roles: What The Bible Says About A Woman's Place In Church And Family.* Michigan: Baker Book House, 1996.

Bitek, Okot P. "Daughters of Africa", Accessed 26 November 97; available from http://www.Africaonline.co.ke; Internet.

Casey, L.K. "Surviving Abuse: Shame, Anger, Forgiveness." *Pastoral Psychology* 46 (March 1998) : 223-231.

Darr, Katheryn P. *Far More Precious Than Jewels: Perspectives On Biblical Women.* Louisville, Kentucky: Westminister/John Knox Press, 1991.

Daly, Mary. *Beyond God The Father: Toward A Philosophy of Women's Liberation.* Boston: Beacon Press, 1973.

Daily Nation (Nairobi, Kenya) 20 December 1996.

_____. Muthui Mwai. 19 July 1998.

Dirie, M.A., and Lindmark, G. "The Risk Of Medical Complications After Female Circumcision." *East African Medical Journal* 69 (January 1992) : 479-483.

Dorkenoo, Efua. *Cutting The Rose. Female Genital Mutilation. The Practice and Its Prevention.* London: Minority Rights Group Publishers, 1995.

_____. *Female Genital Mutilation: Proposals For Change.* London: Minority Rights Group Publishers, 1980

"Egyptian Girl Dies after Being Circumcised." *The Independent On Sunday.* 25 August 97. (Cairo, Egypt)

"Female Genital Mutilation." Accessed on 28 October 97; available from *"www.hollyfeld.org/fgm/africa.html; Internet.* Paul, Bimal, K., "Maternal Mortality In Africa: 1980-87." *Social Science & Medicine: An International Journal* 37 (September 1993) : 745-753.

"FEMISA." Accessed on 11 November 97; available from *"Owner-beijing95-1@netcom.com; Internet.*

Figley, Charles R. *Helping Traumatized Families.* San Francico: Jossey-Bass Publishers, 1989.

Fortune, M.M. *Sexual Violence. The Unmentionable Sin. An Ethical And Pastoral Perspective.* Ohio: Pilgrim Press, 1983.

Gaebelein, F.E. *The Expositor's Bible Commentary. Volume 2. Genesis.*

Grand Rapids, Michigan: Zondervan Publishing House, 1990.

Glaz, M., Moessner, S. *Women In Travail And Transition. A New Pastoral Care.* Minneapolis: Fortress Press, 1991.

Grenz, S.J and Kjesbo, M.D. *Women In The Church: A Biblical Theology Of Women In Ministry.* Downers Grove, Illinois: Inter-Varsity Press, 1995.

Goldman, Ronald. *Circumcision: The Hidden Trauma. How An American Cultural Practice Affects Infants And Ultimately Us All.* Boston: Vangaurd Publications, 1997.

Hastings, Adrian. *Christian Marriage In Africa.* Nairobi, Kenya: Uzima Press, 1974.

Herman, Judith, L. *Trauma and Recovery: The Aftermath of Violence from Domestic Abuse to Political Terror.* New York: Basic Books, 1997.

Hite, Shere. *The Hite Report. A Nationwide Survey Of Female Sexuality.* New York: MacMillan Publishing Company, 1976.

Hosken, F.P. *The Hosken Report. Genital And Sexual Mutilation Of Females.* Lexington, MA: Women's International Network News, 1993.

Jordan, Merle R. *Taking On The gods: The Task Of The Pastoral Counselor.* Nashville: Abingdon Press, 1986.

Joseph, Cathy. "Compassionate Accountability: An Embodied Consideration of Female Genital Mutilation." *Journal of Psychohistory* 24 (Summer, 1996) : 2-17.

Kariara, J, and Kitonga E. *An Introduction to East African Poetry.* Nairobi, Kenya: Oxford University Press, 1976.

Karen, Robert. "Shame." *The Atlantic Monthly*, 2 February 1992, 50-60.

Kato, Byang H. *Biblical Christianity In Africa.* Achimota, Ghana: ACP Press, 1985.

Kaufman, Gershen. *Shame: The Power of Caring.* Cambridge, MA: Schenkman Books, 1985.

Knox, Kay. "Women's Identity: Self Psychology's New Promise." *Women And Therapy* 4, (Fall 1985) : 57-69.

Lowenstein, Sophie. "An Overview of Some Aspects of Female Sexuality." *Social Casework* (February 1978) : 106-115.

_____. "Attitudes And Attitude Differences To Female Genital Mutilation In The Sudan: Is There A Change On The Horizon?." *Social Science & Medicine* 12, (September 1978) : 417-421.

"Mass Female Genital Mutilation in Sierra Leone." *Reuters News Agency.* 12 January 97.

Mambo, G.K., Barret, D.B., Mclaughlin, J., and McVeigh, M.J. *Kenya Churches Handbook. The Development of Kenyan Christianity 1498-1973*. Kisumu, Kenya: Evangel Publishing House, 1973.

Maendeleo Ya Wanawake Organization. *A Report On Harmful Practices That Affect The Health Of Women And Their Children In Kenya*. Nairobi, Kenya: 1982.

_____. *Qualitative Research Report On Female Circumcision In Four Districts In Kenya*. Nairobi, Kenya: 1996.

Manlowe, Jennifer.L. *Faith Born Out Of Seduction. Sexual Trauma, Body Image, And Religion*. New York: New York University Press, 1995.

Mbugua, Judy. *Our Times Has Come. African Christian Women Address The Issues Of Today*. Grand Rapids, Michigan: Baker Book House, 1994.

Murray, Jocelyn M. "The Kikuyu Female Circumcision controversy, With Special Reference to The Church Missionary Society's Sphere of Influence." Ph.D. diss., University of Michigan, 1974.

Nathanson, D.L. *Shame And Pride. Affect, Sex, and the Birth Of The Self*. New York: W.W. Norton & Company, 1992.

Ng'weno, Hilary. "Sexism In Kenya." *The Weekly Review*. Kenya Times Media Trust, August 1991.

_____. "Signs Of The Times?." 18 July 1988.

Njambi, E. M. "Female Circumcision: Why It Should Not Happen." *Parents Magazine,* 1 February 991, 16.

Njoya, Timothy M. *"Out of Silence" A collection of Sermons*. Nairobi, Beyond Magazine Publishers, 1987.

N'thamburi, Zablon. *The African Church At The Crossroads. Strategy For Indigenization*. Nairobi, Kenya: Uzima Press, 1991.

Nichols, P.M, and Schwartz, C.R. *Family Therapy. Concepts And Methods*. Boston: Simon and Schuster Publishers, 1991.

Oduyoye, Mercy. *Hearing And Knowing: Theological Reflections On Christianity In Africa*. New York: Orbis Maryknoll Publishers, 1986.

Olanyika, K.T. *The Circumcision Of Women. A Strategy For Eradication.* Troubleridge-Wiltshire, United Kingdom: Dotasios Publishers, 1992.

_____. *Daughters Of Anowa. African Women And Patriarchy.* New York: Mary Knoll Publishers, 1995.

"Origin Of Circumcision". Accessed 11 November 1997; available from *http://www.fgm; Internet.*

Okullu, Henry. *Church And Marriage In East Africa.* Nairobi, Kenya: Imani House Act Print Limited, 1976.

Omar-Hashi, Kowser. "Female Genital Mutilation: Perspectives From A Somalian Midwife." *Birth: Issues In Perinatal Care* 21 (December 1994) : 224-225.

Poling, Newton J. *The Abuse of Power. A Theological Problem.* Nashville: Abingdon Press, 1991.

Rushwan, Hawid. *"Female Circumcision" World Health.* Geneva, Switzerland: World Health Organization Publication, 1990.

Shaw, Evelyn. "Female Circumcision, What Kind Of Maternity Care Do Women Need? And Can United States Caregivers Provide It?." *American Journal of Nursing.* (June 1985): 684-687.

Shorten, Allison. "Female Circumcision: Understanding Special Needs. *Holistic Nursing Practice* 9 (January 1995) : 66-73.

Tamez, Elsa. "The Woman Who Complicated the History of Salvation." Tr. Betsy Yeager. *In the New Eyes for Reading.* Eds. John S. Pobee and Barbel von Wartenberg-Potter. Oak Park, Ill.: Meyer-Stone Books, 1986

Toubia, Nahid. "Female Circumcision As a Public Health Issue." *The New England Journal of Medicine* 331 (Fall 1994) : 712-716.

Thubi, Abedinego, Gikuyu Tribal Elder. Interview by author, 15 June 1982, Gatura Village, Kenya. Tape recording. High School Oral Literature Project Interview On Gikuyu Customs.

United States Congress Bill Prohibiting Female Genital Mutilation. Accessed 7 October 98; available from http://www.eskimo.com/ gburlin/female.html; Internet.

Walker, Alice, and Pratibha Parmar. *Warrior Marks. Female Genital Mutilation and the Sexual Blinding of Women.* Florida: Harcourt Brace & Company, 1996.

Wanjiku, Mukabi, Jacqueline A. Oduol and Maria Nzomo. *Democratic Change in Africad: Women's Perspective.* Nairobi, Kenya: ACTS Gender Institute, 1993.

White, P.C. *The Cry Of Tamar: Violence Against Women And The Church's Response.* Minneapolis: Fortress Press, 1995.

Whitefield, Charles. L. *Memory and Abuse: Remembering and Healing the Wounds of Trauma.* Deerfield Beach, Florida: Health Communications Publishers, 1995.

World Health Organization. *A Joint WHO/UNICEF/UNFPA Statement.* Geneva, 1997.

Printed in the United States
202739BV00004B/198/A

9 781591 605614